Losing

Patience

Losing Patience

By

Joyce Faulkner

Red Engine Press
P.O. Box 6255
Key West, FL 33040

"Chance" first published by 'One Thousand Whispers', Summer, 2003

"Fatty Mattie" first published by 'Clever Magazine', Summer, 2003

Library of Congress Cataloging-in-Publication data is available upon request.

ISBN 0-9745652-4-5

Cover design and illustrations by Dianna C. Faulkner
Edited by Beth Lieberman

Printed in the United Stated of America

Quantity discounts are available on bulk purchases of this book for educational institutions or social organizations. Any of these stories may be re-printed for specific needs. For information, please contact
Red Engine Press
P.O. Box 6255
Key West, FL 33040.

To

Pvt. Rusty Schneider, USMC

&

Jim Kozumplik

Acknowledgements

I wonder about things that most other folks accept without question. This habit sometimes puts me at odds with my companions. Ideologues don't like challenges to their cherished beliefs. Skeptics find my more imaginative explorations troubling. Fortunately, I have many friends of both persuasions who endure my obsessive ponderings with amused patience. Sometimes I wonder about them.

In particular, these creative spirits engage, challenge and push me -- my dear husband John, my daughter Carmel, my son Nate, my cousin Karen Scott and my editor Beth Lieberman. I also have a cadre of fellow ponderers who graciously allow me to run exotic concepts past them -- Mindy Philips Lawrence, Helen Jones, John Conti, Mark Exlos, Bobby Blades, Mike Van Thiel, Ken Goldberg, J.D. Gordon, Maggie Abbot, Bill Ward and S. Dale "Sierra" Seawright. Thank you all for your ideas, your hard work and your friendship.

Stories in this Collection

Key West Dreams

Jay's stomach rolled as a wave rocked the small boat.

"Are you okay?" Robin squeezed his shoulder.

He nodded.

"Ready?" Ara struggled to keep her balance while hugging the urn to her bosom.

"Do it." He tried to keep the irritation out of his voice. Jim's last bad joke was a doozie.

Ara dumped the ashes overboard.

Jay choked on the warm sea breeze, his eyes watering. It had been six months since his brother's heart attack. Time made grief bearable, but this weird get-together brought everything back.

Robin took his hand. "What does Jim want us to do now?"

"Who knows? He was an odd bird."

Ara blew her nose. "He said you should enjoy Key West." She smiled at Robin and shrugged. "Who else would leave a will like that?"

Ara's hair blazed in the sunlight. Jay closed his eyes, disgusted with himself. It was one thing to lust after his brother's girlfriend, quite another to fantasize about his widow seconds after she had scattered his ashes.

"I have to admit, I never heard of anyone making arrangements like this. In my family, we have a showing at the funeral home and then a mass and then a service at the cemetery." Robin sat on a bench under the canopy pulling Jay down beside her. "Compared to Jim, we are a pretty dull lot."

"He always wanted you guys to come down here," Ara said as though that explained things. "It was his dream."

"So much for dreams." Jay snorted.

"Ignore him." Robin dug her elbow into his side. "He doesn't like to travel."

"Jim wanted you and Jay to do this with me for a reason." Ara put the lid back on the urn and turned her eyes to the horizon as though she was taking Robin's advice.

"He wanted to bust my ass one more time."

"Jay!"

He crossed his arms and rested his chin on his chest. They hadn't been in Key West a day and Robin was already pissed at him. "Sorry," he grunted.

"I didn't tell you. There is one more thing." Ara gestured for their guide to start the engine. "We are supposed to meet Red Canary at Sloppy Joe's for lunch."

"Who the hell is Red Canary?"

"A friend of Jim's." Ara tucked the urn into her big straw purse and sat down, facing away from the water. "A pilot."

"I don't like this." Jay whispered in Robin's ear as they chugged back toward Key West.

• • • • •

"It'll be okay. We'll find something." Robin patted his knee under the table.

"What's a conch?"

"Seafood."

"God." He laid the menu face down on the table.

"Don't get revved up."

"He's still doing it."

"He was just being big brother, Jay."

"I like what I like. Why try anything else?"

"It's just one day." Robin sighed. "One meal! It won't kill you."

The bartender followed Ara with his eyes as she came back from the bathroom. A tourist grinned and fanned himself with his hat as she passed. Jay tried not to notice. "They have great margaritas here," she said as she draped her flowered shawl over the back of her chair. "And Jim loved their calamari."

"What's calamari?" Jay muttered to Robin.

Robin's whisper was hoarse. "Squid."

"I'll have a beer."

Ara picked up the menu. "Why don't you try a hot dog?"

"I don't like hot dogs."

Robin ran her finger down the list of entrees. "The Ernie Burger will work, hon -- if you tell them to hold the cheese."

Exasperated by Robin's whiny concern, he spun on her. "I'M NOT HUNGRY, OKAY?"

Robin flinched and his irritation drained away. "Oh baby, I'm sorry. I didn't mean that."

"I think I'll go back to the hotel." She fumbled with her purse.

He reached for her arm. "There's no need to go. I'll behave."

"I need some space, Jay -- and so do you." Robin jerked her arm away and walked out onto Duval Street.

"Don't forget! Mallory Square at sunset." Ara called out.

"I'll be there." Robin wiggled her fingers over her shoulder and disappeared into the crowd.

Jay and Ara sat across from each other. "I'm a pig."

"No you aren't. You're having a hard time with Jim's death. So am I."

"Robin didn't deserve that."

"So, make it up to her." Ara waved the waitress over to their table. "I'll have a Rum Runner and conch fritters."

The waitress nodded and looked at Jay.

"Ernie burger. No cheese. Bud light?"

"There now. That wasn't so bad, was it?"

He felt Ara's smile in the pit of his stomach. He'd been in love with her all his adult life. His eyes dropped to her fingers thinking about the time he loaned Jim the money to buy her engagement ring.

She closed her hand, rubbing her bare ring finger with her thumb. Shocked, he looked up. "I'm sorry. I was just thinking about -- wondering -- ?"

"I haven't been able to wear it for years -- not since Audrey was born. I was only seventeen when he gave it to me. It's a size four. Funny, I don't remember being that tiny." She pulled a chain out of her bodice. "When Jim was alive, I kept it in a jewelry box -- but the day after he died, I dug it out and I've been wearing it ever since."

He reached out to touch the ring. "He was always a rebel. Who else would give a girl a red diamond?"

Ara wiped the corner of her eye with her knuckle. "It's a ruby, Jay."

"Robin would have killed me if I gave her anything but a diamond."

"I know." She tucked the ring back inside of her blouse.

"There you are." A brawny, red-faced man jerked Ara to her feet and gave her a bear hug.

Jay scowled and stood up, his fists clenched.

"Red!" Ara wrapped her arms around his neck and kissed his cheek. "I've missed you."

"It doesn't seem right seeing you without that crazy husband of yours." He held her close for a moment before turning to Jay. "You must be Jimmy's baby brother. You look just like him."

Stung, Jay blurted out, "He took after the Manakin side of the family. I look like our mother."

Ara stepped gracefully into the awkward silence that followed. "Jay, this is Red Canary. He was Jim's best friend."

"No, now that's not true. I was his best friend in Key West. Jimmy thought the world of you, Jay."

Irritated with this stranger's obvious familiarity with Ara, Jay bit back the urge to explain that his brother's name was Jim, not Jimmy. "It's nice to meet you, Mr. Canary."

"It's Aloysius, actually. But everyone calls me Red."

The waitress appeared with Ara and Jay's drinks and they all sat down.

Red patted his middle. "I'll have plain old Coca Cola on the rocks and a bowl of chili since I'm flying this afternoon."

"What kind of plane do you fly?" Jay took a sip of his beer.

"A 1946 Waco. A biplane. I give people tours of the Keys in it. That's how I met Jimmy. He showed up wanting to fly the Waco. I asked for his credentials and he explained that he had fourteen hours toward his ticket. I about fell outta my chair laughing. Hell, I have fourteen hours upside down!"

"Jim had a lot of nerve." Jay had been hearing stories about Jim's adventures all his life.

5

"I got such a kick outta our Jimmy that I took him up and let him fly her. Got to be a regular thing. That crazy sonofagun was doing aerobatics the day before he died."

The thought of a man with heart disease flying an airplane made Jay queasy. How many other pilots could drop dead on you? The trip back to Pennsylvania suddenly got more stressful. The hair on his arms bristled and he looked up, catching Ara watching him. "What?"

"He thought you'd love it, Jay."

His heart pounded. "NO."

"He made all the arrangements. It's his last wish." Her eyes transfixed him. The damned woman knew what she did to him. She'd always known -- and he'd always known that she knew. Jim knew too. That was the ultimate humiliation -- the winner's awareness of the loser's chagrin.

"I'm not doing it." He folded his arms over his chest. "He can yank my chain from the grave all he wants -- but I'm not going for it."

The waitress brought their food. Welcoming the intrusion, Jay lifted the top bun off his burger and picked out the lettuce and pickles. He replaced the bread and cut the sandwich in two. Not a trace of pink. No mustard. No catsup. He relaxed and took a bite. "This is a great place," he said with his mouth full.

"He wanted to share something with you." Ara wasn't giving up.

"He knew very well what I want." It slipped out between bites and hung in the air between them. He flushed and stole a peek at Red who was polite enough to stare into his chili bowl.

Ara lowered her voice. "That wasn't his to give."

He ducked his chin. "I'm a pig."

She shook her head. "You are anything but that."

"I better go."

6

She laid her hand on his wrist. "Wait."

"I need to make up with Robin," he said but made no effort to leave.

"Let me start over?"

He nodded. Nothing was going to tear him away as long as Ara was touching him.

"Perhaps Jim knew he didn't have a lot of time. His will was elaborate -- generous in unique ways. It was more than a disposition of his belongings. He gave each of us something of himself -- something that touched on who we are and what he felt for us."

"Jim was like that." Jay remembered lying in a field for hours when he was ten while Jim pointed out the constellations. "Whenever he learned something, he got so excited about it that he couldn't stand my not knowing it too."

Ara removed her hand from his wrist. "He told me once that I'd never really know him unless I went up with him. I was scared to death. We were squeezed together in the front cockpit." She closed her eyes. "I could smell his aftershave until we took off. I remember that the engine was loud -- so loud that we couldn't hear each other even though we were only inches apart. I could feel the vibrations through the fuselage -- and his body. We bounced into the air and the wind took my breath away. Key West sparkled beneath us. We stuck out our tongues to taste the air." She opened her eyes. "It's hard to explain, but I felt so alive."

He stared at his wrist, her fingerprints a faint memory. "It sounds lovely."

"Jim was a sensual man. His appreciation of things -- life, the world, me -- was visceral. He enjoyed every bit of it. How could I resist a man like that?"

Jay's erogenous zones tingled. Ara made flying in an airplane sound delicious -- like illicit sex. He thought about his conventional life with his conventional wife -- safe, solid and disappointing. It was easy to see why the Manakin brothers'

7

fortunes had diverged. Jim went after what he wanted -- Jay settled for what he could get. Jim was Key West. Jay was McKeesport. Jay had accepted that truth thirty years ago when Ara walked down the aisle into his brother's arms. Still, just once, it would be nice to be a chiseled-jaw hero who got the girl of his dreams.

He stole another peek at Red who grinned and raised his glass of Coca Cola. A balding middle-aged guy with a big belly and a bad haircut, Red didn't seem exceptional in any way. If HE could fly, surely Jay could do it. After all, it WAS his brother's last gift.

•••••

Terror churned in Jay's stomach. The world slowed down around him as he got into Red's shiny yellow Jeep. Ara hurried off to meet Robin in Mallory Square. She seemed to be running through half-set Jello.

"Are you a parrot head?" Red's voice was low and distorted, like he was under water.

"Huh?"

Red laughed and shoved a CD into the player. Mellow music snuffed out other sounds. "Ready?"

Jay stared at him with his mouth open. "Okay."

Red released the clutch, jerking Jay's head backwards. A tall good-looking woman with an Adam's apple and a large tattoo on her left bicep stood on the corner of Eaton and Simonton. She waved at him. Struck by the friendliness of Key West ladies, he waved back. Red laughed again and clapped him on the back.

As they accelerated down Palm Avenue, Jay began noticing things -- that his shirt was damp under the arms, that the whole damn key smelled like the ocean, that palms and bougainvillea and banyans lined the road. The closer they got to the airport, the faster his heart beat.

Red drove right up to the Waco. It was smaller than Jay expected -- and orange. He snorted. Jim had a sick sense of humor -- sending him to die in an orange biplane.

"Are you okay?"

"I'm fine." Actually, to his surprise, he WAS fine -- scared out of his mind, but fine.

Red gestured to the plane with his head. "Let's do it."

They pushed the Waco out onto the taxiway. It was so light and flimsy that Jay wondered how it would hold them.

"Watch that you don't hit your head on the top wing." Red's voice was kind. Jay realized that he could walk away and Red would never tell anyone he'd chickened out. Of course, Red would know.

Breathing heavily, Jay put his foot on a roughened patch on the lower wing close to the fuselage and gripped a handle mounted toward the front of the cockpit. He paused -- searching for a reason to get in. He thought of Ara. She could choose any man in the world -- why WOULDN'T she want someone special? Someone who could do what ordinary men wouldn't? Ducking the top wing, he threw a leg over the rim and slid into the seat.

"Put this on." Red handed him a leather helmet. "It's really a headset. You'll be able to hear me but not speak to me."

Jay nodded. The helmet was too loose and he fumbled with the strap.

"Here, let me do that." Red slipped the strap through the buckle and tightened it under Jay's chin. "Don't forget the seat belt."

Jay felt under his thighs. "What's this?" He pulled out a long slim leather strap that looked nothing like modern seatbelts.

"Use the last hole."

"It looks like the belt my grandpa used to keep his pants up."

Red gestured with his hands. "Buckle it."

Trembling, Jay focused on that task. When he finished, Red slipped a pair of goggles over his head. "Do I really need these?"

"Yes."

"I hate having anything on my face."

"Suit yourself -- just don't drop them out of the plane."

Jay waited until he could no longer see Red before ripping the goggles off. The airplane rocked as the older man crawled into the back cockpit. The engine started. Panicked, Jay hyperventilated. It didn't matter what Ara thought about him. It didn't matter what Jim wanted. "I gotta get out of here," he yelled, but Red couldn't hear him. "LET ME OUT."

He tore at the seat belt but it was too late. The Waco was moving.

"You okay up there?"

The words blasted into his consciousness. Where were they coming from? He turned his head as far one way as he could. Another plane was landing at the other end of the runway. He screamed and ducked, only daring to peek when he felt the Waco veering off in another direction. He turned to look the other way. Jim's watery grave beckoned. The sea was as green as Ara's eyes. He gripped the sides of the cockpit.

"This is a tail-dragger. The fuselage tilts upwards so that we can't see anything but the engine and sky when we are on the ground. That means I have to zigzag when I taxi so I can see down the runway."

The explanation reassured Jay enough so that he relaxed his grip on the side of the plane and re-buckled the seat belt.

"I'm lining up for take off."

Jay gritted his teeth.

"Here we go."

The noise grew even louder as they raced down the runway. The rush of air in Jay's face was almost too intense to bear -- and yet it was exhilarating too. He blinked, his eyes watering. A bug hit him on the cheekbone and he cried out in pain. Then, almost like they were in an elevator, they were airborne.

"Put on your goggles," Red said into his ear.

Nodding, he capitulated and slipped them over his helmet. His vision cleared and he could see the ocean below him. The sun was making its way toward the horizon, stippling the water with golden highlights.

"Everyone in Key West gathers in Mallory Square each evening to toast the sunset. We will be the only plane in the air and they'll take pictures of us as we fly by. In order to get over there, I'm going to have to turn left. When I do that, the right wing will go down and the left will go up. If you understand, give me a thumbs up."

The fright associated with take-off subsided, but Jay wasn't sure he was ready to turn. Remembering that Ara was watching, he took a deep breath and held up his thumb.

"Here we go." Red dipped the right wing.

Jay felt like he was lying on his right side. At first, he was afraid that he'd fall out, but then he saw that the depth of the cockpit, the position of the top wing over his head and the seatbelt made that an unlikely possibility. As the Waco turned, he felt the sun on his left cheek. He glanced to his right. Hundreds of people milled around in the square below them. Flashes of light. What was that? Was someone shooting at them?

"They are taking pictures of us." Red reminded him. "They want to see a little action. Are you ready for some tricks?"

Tricks? NO!

The nose of the Waco rose up in front of him. All he could see was sky and the spinning blades of the propeller. They were going straight up. Higher and higher. The sound of the engine changed. They were going slower. Slower.

"OH GOD!" He screamed as the plane literally paused in the air before dropping sideways like a stone. He was sure he was going to die. The image of his wife popped into his head. "Robin! Oh baby, I love you."

The Waco turned nose down and picked up speed. The waves rushed up at him. His eyes bulged. He couldn't think, couldn't talk. The air was warm but he knew the water would be cold. All he wanted was to be back in bed with Robin -- holding her.

The plane shrieked as they dove toward the harbor. "He, he, he." Red chuckled into Jay's ear before pulling the nose of the aircraft up so that they skimmed the surface just as the sun sank into the water. "Bet they got some great pictures that time. Only a few more minutes -- we have to land before dark."

The sky was darker as they climbed upwards. Jay gasped for air. Relief swept through his body. His toes tingled. He wiggled them -- rejoiced in them. Clammy from his own sweat, he savored the sour smell of his body. "He, he, he!" He echoed Red's self-satisfied chuckle.

"We're heading back now." Red informed him. "But I want to show you one more thing -- the trick that Jim loved most." Before he could digest this information, Jay was upside down. Then right side up. Then upside down again.

Shocked, he explored how he felt about the two quick rolls. Instead of being afraid, he was delighted. "I did it," he shouted into the wind. "I did it!"

Feeling as bold and daring as his big brother, Jay knew Ara would be impressed and that felt good -- but now that he'd done it, he didn't CARE if she was impressed. On the other hand, he couldn't wait to get back down and tell Robin what he'd done. She'd be happy for him, but he didn't have to prove anything to her. She loved him even though he could be a pig. Thank God.

Delirious with joy, he held both arms in the air like a daredevil on a roller coaster as Red brought the Waco down toward the airport. The moment the wheels touched the pavement, Jay realized these were the last few moments he'd ever spend with Jim. His euphoria faded and he said his final good-byes as Red taxied the orange Waco toward the hangar.

"JAY!" Robin ran toward them as soon as Red cut the engine.

"Baby, oh baby!" He took her into his arms. "I did it."

"You scared the shit out of me." She smacked his shoulder, furious. "You could have been killed. Why the hell did you do such an idiotic thing?"

He searched for a reason. "I wanted to honor Jim's last wish."

"Hon, I don't want to insult you but Jim was a lunatic."

"I know," he crooned smoothing her hair.

"You never tried any of his crazy crap when he was alive, why would you listen to him now that he's dead?" She sniffed.

"I'm not sure who I am without Jim to react against. Maybe I wanted to see if I was crazy too."

Her anger drained away. "If you wanted to try something new you could have gone for the conch fritters."

"I'm not THAT crazy." He held her close. Over her shoulder, he saw Ara leaning against the fender of her car. She was crying. His heart went out to her. Her loss transcended his fantasies of her. Letting go of Jim meant letting go of Ara too, he realized. Loving Jim was the only thing they ever had in common. He was okay with that, he realized as he kissed the top of Robin's head.

CHANCE

I saw her again last night at long last. A graceful phantom striding across my path -- her long white hair glowing like a beacon in the low beams of my old red Volvo. My erection saluted her resilient beauty. I didn't understand myself -- she had to be seventy-five by now.

My bad leg slipped off the clutch. The car lurched and died. Hannah glanced over her shoulder and her chilly blue eyes met mine. No recognition. She continued across the street with the pace of a much younger woman. I gaped at her with the lust of a much younger man. She disappeared into a house two doors down from the intersection.

I drove to the bare apartment I called home and limped to the fridge to collect my first Bass Ale of the evening. Sitting on a sliver of deck outside my sliding glass doors, I dreamed of Hannah -- my cock rising and falling in cadence with my memories.

My father, Arlen Martindale, found Hannah when I was eighteen. They both said they knew it was love when Hannah burst into the office of my Dad's Mobile Home business and inquired about the 'Sunrise Special'. They were married three weeks later on a Thursday afternoon at the local bowling alley. She never did buy a trailer.

Whatever else you can say about Hannah, she made my father happy. I could see it in the way he touched the flesh of her upper arm. Once, I came home from the bookstore at lunchtime and caught them entwined on the couch. They sat up -- straightening their clothes like guilty teenagers. Dad actually blushed. I pretended not to notice and hobbled into the kitchen for a sandwich.

I never knew what broke them up. One day, eighteen months later, Hannah slipped out before breakfast leaving Dad a note telling him where to send her clothes. We sat at the kitchen table eating oatmeal. When he finished, he stared out the window.

"I'm sorry, Dad." I wished it were okay to hug him.

He shrugged and sipped his coffee. "Back to work." He set the mug down solidly on the counter like a punctuation point.

When Hannah was with Dad that first time, I never really noticed her. She was my step-mom -- no way could she replace my rosy-faced mother who died when I was ten. Mostly I ignored her.

Then one day she came into the bookstore. It was November 14, 1962 -- a rainy Wednesday morning. She shook water out of the plastic babushka women wore to protect their bouffant hairdos in those days. Her hair was dark brown then -- twisting and swirling around the crown of her head. Stiff springy bangs decorated her forehead just above her jeweled glasses.

"Hi, Chance. Why don't we do lunch?"

"Me?" My glasses slid down my nose. I pushed them up with a band-aid covered finger.

"You think you could make time for me?" I noticed her pointy breasts under her pink sweater along about then. She was a little taller than me, but in her spike-heeled shoes I stared at her lips and chin mostly. My heart pounded.

I held a broken-spined umbrella over us and struggled to keep up with her long legged stride. We found a corner booth at Maxine's Café two blocks from the bookstore. I ordered lemonade with my sandwich -- she drank hot tea.

"Chance, I need you to bring me some papers from Arlen's desk. I feel funny about calling him given the situation." She leaned forward and her nipples grazed the table.

"What do you need?" My eyes caressed her bosom.

"There's an envelope marked "Insurance" in the middle drawer. I put all my tax records in it. We're coming up on the end of the year, so I'm going to need them."

"Okay."

"Are you paying attention, Chance? Yes, I see that you are." She pulled her slant-eyed, black-framed glasses off and laughed, rocking her shoulders to make her breasts jiggle.

I suddenly realized what she was saying. I had been rude. "Oh Hannah, I'm sorry." I blubbered.

"How old are you?"

"Twenty. Almost twenty." I stared at my hands, the tips of my ears burning.

"You look so much younger -- no trace of a beard." She reached across the table and touched my cheek. I flinched. "Have you ever had a woman, Chance?"

I shook my head.

"Why not?"

"I don't know. My leg..." I shrugged.

"This is one sport where you don't need your leg, buddy." I peeked up at her through my lashes. She winked.

"Okay, let's go, big boy." Leaving five dollars on the table to pay for lunch, she stood and held out her hand to me. When I didn't take it, she slipped her fingers through mine and pulled me to my feet. I was breathing heavily.

The windshield wipers bumped back and forth on her green fifty-six Chevy as we turned down an overgrown, muddy path just outside of town. She parked under a pine tree.

16

Even now, I remember she smelled like warm vanilla and her body quivered when I touched it. I couldn't get over that. It was pretty heady stuff -- a grown woman giving herself to me. Thirty years later, I can't breathe when I think about it.

When it was over, she pinched my cheek and laughed. "Now he's a great big man, isn't he?"

I looked away. She used the rearview mirror to retouch her makeup and pat stray sprigs of hair back into the beehive.

"We better get you back home." She put the car in reverse and backed around the tree. Staring out the window as we headed for town, I sniffed my hand from time to time. She pulled up in front of the bookstore.

"Thanks, Hannah." I didn't know what else to say.

A week later, she went back to Dad. There she was at breakfast, eating oatmeal with us. I glanced from one to the other. Neither of them offered an explanation. I'd never got around to taking her that envelope.

Dad was happy again. He went to work late and came home early. Hannah met him at the door and threw her arms around his neck. He squeezed her buttocks with thick-fingered hands as if he were staking a claim. One night, he came into the living room where I sat reading and winked like he knew a secret I didn't. Hannah followed him into the room. She looked at me, her mouth twitching at the corners.

Most nights I lay in bed trying to block out the image of him taking her. I pulled a pillow over my head to drown out the muffled moans and slow squeaking sounds coming from his room. Standing naked in front of my mirrored closet door, I examined my deficiencies. A thin, white manikin with one leg longer than the other, I leaned to the right like some Italian Tower. I was too young and crippled to compete.

Every morning, Dad and I left the house while Hannah stayed home to do whatever it was she did. She quit her job as an Insurance Agent the same day she came back. That must have pleased Dad. He whistled as he drove me to work.

17

I priced and stacked books pretending she wanted me. I ran the register dreaming she'd come back for me, not him. It was hopeless. I grew to hate my own father.

I fancied I was no longer welcome at the dinner table. He wanted to be alone with his prize. The three of us sat quietly in the candlelight. Hannah focused on Dad -- filling his plate with the best morsels -- asking after his health -- gazing at him with the eyes of a newlywed. Once in a while, she'd glance at me. I hated her too.

Then, Dad had to go to market to pick out which units 'Martindale Mobile Homes' would offer in the spring of 1963. He packed his bags, kissed Hannah one last lingering time and was off for the big city.

Hannah drove me to work. Before I got out of the Chevy, she ran her long-nailed fingers inside my thigh and peered at me over her glasses. That evening, I came home to Hannah and took Dad's place in her bed. The whole night was mine. I acted out every fantasy Hannah had ignited that November afternoon in the woods.

"Oh Chance!" She moaned under my lips. "I've wanted you so much. I came back for you. It was always you. I've endured him to get back to you."

Filled with the passion of youth, I believed her. I wanted to believe.

"Will you marry me?" I sat on the side of the bed, rubbing my bad leg, her scent clogging my mind.

"I'm already married, Chance." She sighed. "If only I'd met you first."

"You can leave him. You did once."

"How do you think he would feel if I left him for you? It would hurt him. If I could only do it without him knowing." Hannah knelt behind me on the bed, her breasts pressing against my back. Her flesh stirred me again. I was only twenty. Her tone sounded right to me then.

I left her curled up naked under the quilt my grandmother made for my mother's hope chest. Her glasses lay on the nightstand along with her Timex and a two-month old 'Glamour' magazine. For all our athletic lovemaking, her upswept hairdo remained in place, her make-up untouched. Her snore was a soft 'brrrrrr' as I closed the door behind me.

I hopped downstairs and took three bottles of Dad's Budwiser out of the old Kelvinator. The first one made a satisfying 'pop' and then 'sssss' when I opened it. I went out onto the back porch and sat in a painted lawn chair trying to remember I loved my Dad. He coached little league all those years when I was a kid. Of course, I was never able to play. I was just the batboy. I opened the second beer and sniffed my fingers. The thought of him savoring that sweetness enraged me. He was an experienced player. I couldn't bat against him directly. I needed subterfuge and a fury fueled by testosterone and madness. Turns out I had plenty of both.

The next night I beat Arlen Martindale to death with a baseball bat when he came home. I remember the look on his face when I first swung. When he was dead, I limped over to the couch and sat down. Blood spatters covered the walls -- and me. I shuddered. Hannah called the police.

I went willingly to prison. I was numb -- my passion for Hannah died with my father -- splashed on the floor in our hallway. She never came to see me anyway. She owned the house my father built when I was a baby. She put her things in my Mother's hope chest. She even inherited 'Martindale Mobile Homes.'

I served two years before I realized Hannah intended to kill Dad for insurance and I was her weapon. In the thirteenth year of my sentence, I understood there are all kinds of passion.

It took ten years to find her after I got out of prison. After all, she could live anywhere she pleased. She took out two million dollars in whole life before she left him the first time. When Arlen Martindale died, it was double indemnity -- no questions asked. I was small and boyish, crippled -- a loner. No one guessed she used me. Not even me. They thought I went crazy on my own.

I sat on the deck, my legs dangling through the railing, sucking down beer after beer. At midnight, I threw my bat into the back of the Volvo and drove to her house. I parked on a side street. Holding the bat inside my coat, I crept up to her door and rang the bell.

The porch light came on.

"Who is it?" Her voice had deepened with age and cigarettes.

"Chance Martindale." I was no longer skinny. My black hair had thinned on top. I wore contacts and an orthopedic shoe. I was erect and straight. I looked normal.

She opened the door smiling. Her nipples glowed through the sheer fabric of her nightgown. She was confident of her allure -- even now. Maturity was subtle in her face. Soft lines radiated from her eyes and her lips. A slight stoop in her shoulders was the only concession her body made to age. Her snowy white hair shimmered in the moonlight when I first swung the bat.

ANDREW

1865

Grover Bell was exhausted. Dense foliage and early morning ground fog hid the horizon on three sides. To the south, the land sloped down to a small creek. He limped to the bank and lay flat on his belly to drink. Dipping his hat in the stream, he jammed it back on his head and shivered as the cold water trickled down his neck. Refreshed, he sat up and removed the dirty bandage -- soaking days of dried blood, pus and road grit from his foot.

He'd lasted nearly three years. In battle after battle, men fell to the right and left of him, but he never got a scratch. Then on the way home, months after his boots disintegrated, he stepped on a thorn. The foot was grossly swollen, red and warm to the touch. He leaned forward and sniffed. An odd sweet smell. Puzzled, he rewrapped the wound with the remains of his last shirt.

Resting against a rock, he poked through his knapsack -- a couple of over-soft pears and bits of stale johnnycake. Some coffee but no sugar. He looked around. The woods were full of birds and squirrels -- maybe deer. He checked his pockets. Not much ammunition left. Hunting would be limited.

Leaning on the musket, he struggled to stand. The pain was excruciating. He couldn't walk any further. Looking around, he realized there were worse places to rest. He'd stay one day. Fishing wouldn't take much effort. He'd cook up a mess of crappie. Finish the last of the coffee. Sleep.

Happy with his decision, he hobbled into the woods to cut a fishing pole. He was chopping through the base of a sapling with the bayonet when he heard a horse in the distance. Crouching behind a bush, he watched a young man in a blue uniform ride into the clearing.

"We're lost, Maggie." The soldier swung down out of the saddle and wrapped the reins around a branch. "Maybe I can see the road from that tree over there."

The little red mare dipped her lips delicately into the stream. Was there food in her saddlebags? Grover watched the soldier hoist himself up into a sturdy fork in the tree. Poised about twenty feet off the ground, the young man surveyed the valley beyond the rocks. Sweating and feverish, Grover's eyes drifted back to the horse.

With a horse, he would be sitting in his mother's kitchen eating beans and cornpone within a week. With a horse, the foot would have a chance to heal. If all else failed, he could trade her for food -- or a train ticket home. He picked up the musket and hopped out of the thicket.

Maggie whinnied when she saw him. "Hold on, girl." Grover patted her neck and wrapped the reins around his left hand.

"What the hell are you doing?" The soldier yelled from his perch twenty yards away.

Grover slipped his infected foot into Maggie's left stirrup. Wincing, he grabbed the saddle with his left hand and tried to throw his other leg over her withers. With the gun in his right hand, he was off balance. The mare jerked away and he fell backwards.

"STOP! THIEF!" The soldier drew his pistol and slid down the trunk of the tree.

Maggie pivoted dragging Grover in a circle. With his foot caught in the stirrup, clinging to the reins with one hand and clutching the musket with the other, he screamed in agony.

The soldier ran toward them. "You stupid ass. Let go!"

Second time around, Maggie slammed Grover's arm against a rock and the musket discharged. The blast caused her to rear up on her hind legs. Grover's foot came out of the stirrup. The horse tossed her head and turned to run, but Grover hung on and after a few steps, she stopped fighting him.

He lay on his back with his eyes closed expecting the soldier to shoot him dead any minute. When the shot didn't come, he turned his head. Through Maggie's legs, he saw a blue form stretched out on the ground less than ten feet away. Rolling onto his side, he raised up on one elbow. The figure didn't move.

Relief washed over him. Death wasn't coming today. It was someone else's turn. Elated that he wouldn't have to fight for the horse, he crawled over to the body on all fours. The ball had hit the trooper just above the right eye.

Hoping there was plenty of ammunition in Maggie's saddlebags, Grover took the pistol. The boots would come in handy once his foot healed. So would the clothes. The blue tunic wasn't new but it wasn't worn out either. In the chest pocket, he found a thick packet of letters addressed to Andrew Pike in a feminine hand.

"Too bad that bullet went for your head and not your heart, Andrew." He sighed. "You'd be alive right now."

Close up, Andrew resembled Grover's cousin Jake. Maybe a year or two younger. Smooth cheeked and as beautiful as a girl. Grover's excitement faded. As far as he knew, this was the first time he'd killed anyone.

Fact was, despite his years at war, Grover never shot at the forces advancing on him. Usually he busied himself loading muskets for those willing to fire. Sometimes he pretended to shoot and reload, jamming four or five balls down the barrel of his musket. When he did pull the trigger, he aimed high. Enemy faces filled with fear and determination looked too much like those of his comrades. He wasn't a coward. In charge after charge, he exposed himself to danger. He didn't mind dying for the cause, he just couldn't bring himself to kill for it.

He stared at the slim body stretched out on the ground. Poor Andrew. It was so stupid. The war was over. To die now -- by accident -- just because he got lost. Was God playing with them? Grover wiped the corner of his eye with the back of his hand.

He had no illusions about death. He'd seen his share of battlefields. Soon Andrew would sour and bloat. Birds and animals would feast on him. Within days, what had been bursting with youth and hope would become horrible with rot -- and this time it was Grover's fault. He owed Andrew -- something -- at least a grave and a few words.

It was late afternoon when he finished burying Andrew. Mud coated his feet and a thin bloody discharge fouled the bandage. He wasn't sure if the pungent smell was Andrew or his own infection. Nauseated, he vomited behind a bush before stripping off his ragged clothes and wading into the creek. The water was cold. Shivering, he rubbed his arms and legs. He wanted to be clean but filth clung to him like an odor.

Andrew's things were too big, but there were no unmended holes. It felt odd wearing the blue uniform, but he guessed they were all brothers again. Sitting on the bank, Grover soaked his foot in the stream while he shaved. Feeling almost human, he consolidated his belongings with Andrew's and repacked Maggie's saddlebags.

Ready to leave, Grover stood over the pile of rocks where he'd buried the body. Taking off Andrew's hat, he held it over his heart and cleared his throat. "Yea, though I walk in a valley." He searched for the words. "God's with us now and at the hour of our death, Amen."

"What's happened to me?" Andrew whispered in Grover's ear.

Maggie screamed and shied.

24

Grover spun around, his eyes bulging at the sight of Andrew's ghost. "You're dead."

The apparition stared at the grave. "I can't be dead. I'm on my way home to get married. Amelia will kill me if I miss the wedding."

Grover clung to the panting mare. "Trust me. I wish it wasn't so, but you are dead."

"NO!" Andrew's agony ripped through Grover's soul. "Please, God. I'll go to church every Sunday. I'll build that barn I've been promising Pa. I want to sleep with Amelia. I want to give my mother a grandchild. I want to carry on the family name. Oh God! Don't take me now. Not yet!"

"I'm sorry." The words slipped out of Grover's mouth unbidden. He knew they were meaningless, yet he needed to say something.

Andrew's pale blue eyes fixed on Grover. "Was it you?"

"No." Unable to look away, Grover shook his head. "It was an accident."

Andrew grabbed Grover by the front of his shirt. "Was it you?"

"I wanted the horse." Grover's eyelids fluttered.

"You damn thief." Andrew slapped him three times. "People are counting on me."

Grover clenched his fists. "I can't change it now."

Andrew's fury drained away. "I know." He sat down on the mound over his grave, his face a mask of despair. "What am I supposed to do?"

"I don't know." Grover grimaced, balancing on one foot. "I thought your soul got sucked up to heaven right off the bat."

"Then why am I here?"

Grover didn't have an answer.

"I can't believe that's me." The ghost stared at the rocks beneath him. "Is this a nightmare?"

"I sure hope so." Grover stroked Maggie's nose. It was soft -- and it was real. "But I don't think it is."

"Who are you?"

"I'm Grover Bell from the Cookeville Bells? In Mississippi?"

"I don't mean your name. I mean, who are you?"

"I'm just a guy trying to get home."

Andrew frowned. "Aren't those my clothes?"

"I didn't figure you'd need them."

"You killed me for my clothes?"

"For the horse." Grover held up the reins.

"So why are you still here?"

"I couldn't leave you like that. It didn't seem right."

"What difference does it make?"

Grover sat down on the rocks next to Andrew. "I don't know. I've been trying to figure that out."

They sat quietly, lost in their thoughts.

"When I was a kid," Grover said. "I had this fear of doing something so bad that no one could ever forgive me -- so bad that I couldn't forgive myself. I guess this is it. Something I'll regret for the rest of my life."

"You arrogant bastard. You think this is about you?"

In fact, Grover did think it was about him. Andrew's problems were over after all.

"What about my family? What about Amelia? If I died in battle, at least the army would notify them. There'd be some record -- but here, in the middle of nowhere -- in an unmarked grave --." The ghost covered his face with his hands and sobbed. "I'll be lost forever."

Grover hadn't considered what it might be like to die out here alone. The idea was horrifying. He searched for something comforting to say. "Maybe it was just your time?"

"And you were God's instrument?" Andrew's sarcasm irritated him.

"Why not? Here we are in this big empty forest -- the only two people in fifty miles and we run into each other?"

"So now you are trying to wiggle out of it?"

"If it was meant to be, then who am I to question it? It was an accident after all."

"An accident that YOU caused."

Grover couldn't get around that part either. "I'm sorry you got killed -- but I'm not sorry about trying to steal Maggie. And I'm not sorry about wanting to get home in one piece." He stood up. "Having said that, I'm not going to stick around here and feel guilty. Whatever's going to happen to you now isn't my fault." Wincing, Grover pulled himself up onto Maggie's back. "Good luck, Andrew. Enjoy whatever God has in store for you."

"Where are you going?"

"Mississippi."

"I'm going with you."

"No." Grover pulled on the reins and Maggie backed away. "I'm leaving you here. I don't want to think about you ever again." He clicked his tongue against his teeth and nudged Maggie's sides with his bare heels. Just as the horse trotted into the thicket, he glanced over his shoulder. The ghost stood on the grave with his hands on his hips, the setting sun flickering through his shade.

"Come on, Maggie. Let's get in a few miles before nightfall." They emerged from the forest and galloped across a wide valley. The sweet smell of the earth chased away the stench of gunpowder. Maggie laboring between his thighs, the taste of evening in the wind, the throbbing beat of Grover's

27

heart all built to a crescendo. "I'm alive." He leaned back in the saddle and closed his eyes. "I'm alive, I'm alive, I'm alive." Each time a bullet whizzed past his ear and ripped into someone else, he'd thanked God even as he grieved for the man beside him. It was impossible to feel truly sorry over another soul's destiny when it was the result of your own good fortune. Yes, Andrew was dead -- but Grover was alive and he rejoiced.

Grover slowed Maggie to a trot until he found a place to camp for the night. While she grazed, he gathered a few twigs to start a fire. There was sugar in Maggie's saddlebags -- and some hardtack. He made thick sweet coffee and crumbled the dense cracker into it. Hunger made the food palatable, but after a couple of bites, he set it down. The swelling extended far up his leg now -- looking at it was enough to destroy his appetite.

He'd tucked the packet of letters he found on Andrew's body into the knapsack. Staring into the fire, he examined them again. Stained and discolored, the ink smeared in places -- there were twenty-three envelopes tied together with a string. "My darling Andrew," one of them began. Another ended with, "I wait for you, my love." Between two pieces of wrinkled paper, he found a picture of a plain-faced girl.

Seeing Amelia made Andrew's life seem real. What he'd been -- a chubby baby in his mother's arms, a young man bringing flowers to Amelia, a soldier going off to war. What he'd never be -- a husband, a father, an old man. One stupid moment changed everything. Grover hated Andrew for getting in the way and for dying.

The last paper in the packet wasn't a letter. It was a map, drawn with pencil in a different hand. He held it up to the firelight. A big X marked a spot near what looked like a cabin. Beyond the flames, Andrew's presence loomed like an ugly secret waiting to be revealed.

Grover lay down, propping his head on the saddle. His leg ached. Sadness covered him like a blanket. He fell asleep thinking about his mother and little sister.

When he woke up the next morning, Andrew was sitting beside him.

"Go away."

"I can't."

Grover struggled to sit up. "You can't hang on forever. Just let go."

"I love it all so much."

"I know." Grover stretched his leg. Something crackled on the bottom of his foot. "Me too. But maybe where you are going is even better."

"I thought about that, but I have unfinished business."

"Amelia?"

"I woke up yesterday thinking about Amelia -- about what it would be like to hold her. I wanted to kiss her the day I left, but I was too shy. I was only a boy then. One of my many regrets is that she'll never know me as a man. I haven't seen her in four years. She accepted my proposal by letter. She doesn't need me, Grover. When I don't come home, she'll be heartbroken -- but she'll go on. No, it's not Amelia."

"What then?" Afraid of what he might see, Grover unwound the bandage around his foot.

Andrew laid a ghostly hand on Grover's shoulder. "Maybe it's as you said. There's a reason we bumped into each other."

Grover felt weak. The sole of his foot was turning black and small gas pockets bubbled under the skin. He looked up at Andrew. "It's a terrible thing to die alone."

"Yes," said Andrew. "It is."

"I don't have much time, do I?"

Andrew shook his head. "No."

Grover lay back down, not bothering to rewrap the foot. "DAMN, DAMN, DAMN!"

"You have the map. Maggie can take you there by sunset. Amelia will take care of you."

"When you died, I thought I'd be spared." A tear ran down Grover's yellowing cheek. "I thought God sent you to go in my place -- because, you know, it was your time."

"Come on, Grover." Andrew squatted beside him.

"I'm tired -- so sick. And thirsty, so thirsty."

"It's the fever. Take a sip from the canteen."

Grover fumbled for the water. "You're a ghost. Your suffering is over. Why?"

"If you stay here, no one will ever know what happened to either of us. They'll wait. Maybe for years. But if you find Amelia, she'll know I'm not coming home -- and she'll write to your mother for you."

Grover found the musket and used it to help himself stand. "What if I don't make it?"

"You will." Andrew whistled and Maggie trotted over to them.

Grover's heart was beating way too fast. He leaned his head against the horse's neck. "I killed you, Andrew."

"Death has made us brothers."

Grover climbed into the saddle. "I'm afraid."

"It won't be long now." Andrew said into his ear. "And you won't be alone."

FATTY MATTIE

"Two hundred and forty-eight pounds." The nurse peered through the lower lenses of her bifocals. Mattie glanced over her shoulder. Perhaps no one heard the nurse's pronouncement.

She stepped off the scale and slipped back into her sandals. "These are very heavy shoes."

The nurse scowled.

"Guess you've heard that one before." Mattie disguised her blush with a grin.

"Ten times a day."

"I'm healthy though." She followed the nurse down the hallway to a small room and crawled up on the examination table. "Healthy as a horse."

The woman wrapped the blood pressure cuff around Mattie's arm.

Mattie forced herself to relax. "I get nervous when you do that."

"One ninety over one ten."

Mattie cringed.

"Give me your finger." The nurse unzipped a black case.

"What's that?"

"Glucometer. The doctor wants to check your blood sugar."

Mattie jumped as the nurse pricked her finger and milked a blood drop onto a test strip. The glucometer beeped. "One sixty-five," she read. "Are you sure you didn't eat anything this morning?"

"Nothing." Mattie gave up trying to be merry and dangled her legs over the edge of the examination table, fighting back tears. It was all beginning again.

"The doctor will see you in a moment. By the way, Happy Birthday, Mattie."

"Thanks, Lois."

●●●●●

"Happy Birthday dear Mattie, Happy Birthday to you." The kids gathered around the table as Mattie blew out ten candles.

"Here, sweetheart. Let me cut the cake for you." Her mother whisked the round pink confection into the kitchen.

"Are we having ice cream too?" Ronnie bounced in his seat.

"You bet." Mattie's dad patted her little brother on the back.

"Cherry Chunk?"

"You got it, buddy."

The little boy clapped his hands. "With Chocolate sauce?"

"Here ya go, Mattie. Happy Birthday, darling." Her mother sat a plate with a miniscule slice of the cherry cake in front of her.

"Can't I have ice cream too?" Mattie eyed the syrupy dessert the other kids were eating.

"You're getting a little hefty, kiddo." Her father spooned chocolate drenched ice cream into his mouth. "Wouldn't want anyone to call you Fatty Mattie, would you?"

"Fatty Mattie!" Ronnie laughed with his mouth full.

"Fatty Mattie, Fatty Mattie!" The other kids chanted.

Mattie scowled. "Stop it, Ronnie. Make them stop, Mama."

"Shush! Stop it or I'll take away YOUR ice cream." Her mother called from the kitchen. "I swear, Paul. You act like a kid yourself."

"Well, she IS a little tub of lard. Whose fault is that?" Her father belched and wandered into the den with a second dish of Mattie's birthday cake and ice cream.

Mattie eyed the cake in front of her. It wasn't much more than a bite. "Come on, Mattie. Don't be like that." Her mother sat down with a tiny slice of her own.

"I want what they got." Mattie stuck out her lower lip.

"You know how he is." Her mother whispered. "Don't get him going."

• • • • •

"Hello, Mattie. How have things been?" Doctor Reece shook her hand before sitting down at his desk with her file.

"I'm fine, sir."

He shuffled through the papers in her file. "Things are getting out of hand with your blood pressure, Mattie." He took off his glasses and turned to face her. "Did you ever consider losing weight?"

• • • • •

"You are beautiful."

Mattie stood at the foot of the bed, caressing his foot. "Aw, you are sweet."

He reached out for her. "So slim and trim."

She crawled into bed beside him, covering them both with the sheets. "I love you, Eddie."

"Promise me you'll not get fat like your Mama. Promise me you'll always be beautiful like you are today."

She rolled away from him. "My mother is beautiful."

"Your mother is FAT." He snuggled up behind her.

"That doesn't make her any less beautiful."

He kissed the back of her neck. "No, I suppose it doesn't. I'm sorry, baby. I didn't mean anything by it."

"Yes, you did." She wiped her eyes with the corner of the sheet. It hadn't been an easy transition from chubby little girl to tall, lithesome young woman.

"I was an insensitive clod, Mattie. I didn't mean to criticize your mom. She's a lovely lady. I was trying to make you feel good. I screwed up."

She bit her knuckle and closed her eyes.

• • • • •

"What do you mean, consider?"

"I mean your numbers are lousy. You are fifty-eight years old and a hundred and twenty pounds overweight. Your blood pressure is out of sight and so is your sugar. When's the last time you got any exercise?"

"Today. I climbed the escalator two steps at a time."

"Mattie, this is no laughing matter."

The smile faded from her face. "You think I'm heavy on purpose? Is that what you think?"

"All you have to do is push yourself back from the table."

"Oh? Is that all I have to do?" Her eyes flashed. "You think it's as simple as that?"

"Use more calories than you take in and you will lose weight." The doctor's sigh was long and wheezy. "You lose even a little bit of weight and your sugar will be easier to control. So will your blood pressure."

"Right."

• • • • •

34

She took the potato chips off of her plate and stashed them in her napkin as soon as the waitress walked away. "I'll be right back," she whispered.

"Are you feeling sick again?"

"You know how pregnant women are, Eddie. We have to pee all the time." She squeezed out of the booth and waddled to the bathroom, holding her napkin against her chest.

Someone was in the handicapped stall. Mattie danced from one foot to the other. "Please, please, please." The door swung open and an old woman shuffled to the sinks, using an aluminum walker. Mattie turned sideways to allow her to pass before hurrying into the stall.

Standing over the toilet, Mattie crushed the potato chips inside her napkin. Her nostrils flared at the smell of stale oil. Holding the bundle over the bowl, she dusted the tiny pieces into the water. Relieved to be rid of them, she pressed the chrome handle and watched the water swirl around. "Thank God!" She murmured to herself as she ripped the paper into tiny shreds and flushed them as well.

"I was about to send in the Cavalry to see if you fell in." Eddie bit into his half-eaten burger.

"I needed to get rid of some things." She examined the tuna sandwich trying to decide how much she dared eat.

"You've been throwing up for weeks. You have to eat something." He dunked a fry into a puddle of Heinz Catsup.

"The doctor says I'm gaining too much too fast."

"That doctor is nuts. You can lose it after the baby is born. Besides, you aren't eating enough to keep a Chihuahua alive."

"I know, but look at me. I'm puffed up like a beached whale."

"You worry too much. Eat. Eat!" He gestured toward her sandwich.

She picked up a butter knife. "Maybe half."

The flavor exploded in her mouth. She gulped down the triangle of bread and tuna, in spite of her determination to savor it. Still hungry, she drank a glass of water with a slice of lemon in it. The other half of her sandwich beckoned. Before she lost control, she peeled off the bread and poured a small mound of salt on the tuna.

Eddie rolled his eyes. "How many calories, Mattie?"

It was hard to think. A boiled egg early in the day. Some celery around noon. A glass of milk mid-afternoon. The sandwich. She added up the calories. "Around five hundred."

"You can't live on that."

"I have to. I've gained forty pounds and I'm only five months along."

"Oh come on, no one gains that much weight on what you eat. You must be sneaking food."

Sneaking food? The thought was riveting, but she didn't dare. Once she started eating, it was like sliding down an endless mud bank. She couldn't stop.

● ● ● ● ●

"I recommend you see our nutritionist. She'll get you on the straight and narrow. The appropriate number of calories. The right mix of exercise. You stick to it and you'll see a marked improvement in a short time." The doctor busied himself writing something in her file.

"How many calories?"

"Two thousand."

Mattie snorted. "You have to be kidding! I don't eat that much now."

The doctor raised one eyebrow. "Perhaps you are miscalculating your caloric intake."

She shook her head. "I'm a pro at this, doctor. I've lost a thousand pounds in my lifetime."

He backed down. "Fifteen hundred calories?"

Her laugh was sarcastic. "Get real."

• • • • •

"How much do you normally weigh?" The secretary held a Bic over the form.

"Do you mean what am I supposed to weigh? Or what do I usually weigh?"

The woman didn't smile.

Mattie gave up. "One twenty-five."

"How long since you weighed one twenty-five?"

"Never."

The woman wrote something on the paper. "How much weight do you want to lose?"

Mattie thought for a moment. "If I could get down to one hundred and fifty, I'd be happy."

"Let's see, that's sixty pounds."

Her shoulders sagged. "Yes."

"Let's see, with drugs and daily visits -- four hundred dollars plus food."

"What kind of drugs?"

"A stimulant to keep you going -- and a vitamin shot once a week. You'll need to be monitored every day while you're eating less than one thousand calories."

"How low will I go?"

"Six hundred calories."

"Ha! No sweat."

• • • • •

Doctor Reece leaned back in his chair. "How many times have you tried, Mattie?"

"I started out with Weight Watchers in the early seventies. Lost twenty-four pounds after our first baby and kept it off ten months. Then I got pregnant again."

"Gained too much?"

"Lost too much. Ended up in the hospital. Gained too much while nursing. Then I went to a Bariatric Center and lost forty-two pounds."

• • • • •

"You look GOOD!" The man kissed her lips so quickly that she stepped back in surprise.

"Don't." She looked around for Eddie who was filling his plate at the buffet table.

He crowded her into the corner. "Something's different about you. I'm not sure what. New make-up? No, not that. New perfume?"

"Stop it." She stamped her foot and wriggled away giggling, embarrassed and flattered at the same time.

"Oh, I have it now." He held up one finger. "You are the one who used to be so fat."

• • • • •

"If you go to such trouble to lose it, why do you gain it back?"

"I have to focus on it all the time."

"What?"

"It takes all my energy to lose weight. One time, I lost seventy pounds eating little packets of designer foods and exercising three times a day. It took almost two years. It's all I thought about. It took all of my attention not to gain -- and so, when shit happened, I lost my focus and it crept back."

"What kind of shit?"

"My mother died."

• • • • •

The heart monitor danced, wide sweeping peaks crashing into deep troughs. The beeping increased. Mattie touched her mother's hand. It felt like cold butter, the fingernails turning blue.

"Oh Mama," Mattie sobbed.

Her mother relaxed into the hospital bed, her mouth dropping open and her eyes staring upwards. Mattie backed away as her father and brother crowded around the body. Not sure if it was terror or grief that impelled her, she ran down the hall and into the courtyard -- taking deep breaths, not yet ready to cry.

She found her way through the gate and jogged down the street to the park. Finding the track, she ran -- her ponytail swinging behind her, her tennis shoes making soft plopping sounds on the pavement. She breathed through her mouth, pumping her arms.

Then she heard it -- her own heart beating -- bubump, bubump. She visualized the jagged lines marching across her mother's monitor. Bubump, bubump. Her pulse quickened. She rounded the corner and stopped, leaning over to put her hands on her knees.

• • • • •

"So you stopped exercising?"

"Not all at once. I worked out until I felt my heart beating. Then I'd get scared and stop. Sometimes I'd hear it beating while I was still in bed in the morning."

The doctor assumed an authoritarian tone. "You treat it like a project. It's a lifestyle change. Fruits, vegetables. Small portions. Not a diet." He made check marks in her file. "If you gain a little one week, work on losing it the next."

"My record is twelve pounds gained in one week -- that would take six weeks to lose." Mattie laughed. "Not even Doctor Atkins can lose it any faster."

"You can't give up."

His arrogant naiveté amused her. "No? Why can't I? Why can't I be like everyone else and eat when I'm hungry?"

• • • • •

Her stomach rumbled. Eddie snorted and rolled onto his side. Slipping into an XX Large fleece robe, she crept down the stairs. She'd been fasting for a week. The first two days she drank pineapple juice -- then just distilled water. Her head pounded. The roast she'd made Eddie and the boys for dinner sat in the fridge. The light came on when she opened the door.

She reached for it, her hands quivering in the air. She put them in her pockets and squatted. The meat was lovely -- pink at the center. She imagined how it would feel in her mouth. She closed the refrigerator door. Her longing was intense. She took a loaf of Roman Meal out of the pantry, coated the heel with strawberry jelly and sprinkled brown sugar over it. She made the second one while she was cramming the first into her mouth.

The nausea was instantaneous. She threw up into the sink, running water to hide her retching.

"Don't think you are hiding anything from me." Eddie was sitting at the kitchen table when she turned around, wiping her mouth on her sleeve.

She sank into a chair and laid her head on the table. "You must be so disappointed in me."

"Mattie, look at me."

"I'm listening." She was too ashamed to look up.

"This has to stop. You are driving me crazy."

"I know." She studied her hands. Her wedding rings no longer fit.

"One of these days, I'm going to find you stretched out across the floor with x's on your eyes."

"Maybe that would be the best thing."

"Mattie!"

"I know I disgust you. I disgust myself. I'm not the slim woman you wanted."

"Did I ever say that?"

"Sort of." She pulled a tissue out of her robe pocket and blew her nose.

He reached across the table to take her hand. "Why do you think I'm still here?"

"I've always wondered that. All my life, wherever we went, I was with the sexiest man in the room. How awful it must be for you to have only me."

"Look at me, Mattie. Really look at me. I'm middle aged with my own paunch. I'm balding and my jowls sag. Hell, I even got hair growing in my ears. I'm no Kevin Costner."

She raised her eyes. "That's not true, Eddie. You are the most beautiful man I've ever known."

"And you are still that beautiful girl I married so long ago." He squeezed her hand. "Enough of this, Mattie. Relax. Enjoy your life."

• • • • •

She wrung her hands. "I finally made peace with myself, doctor. I accepted my lot -- learned to appreciate who I am. Now you are making it all matter again."

The doctor cleared his throat. "This isn't about how you look. It's about your health. I can treat your blood pressure and the diabetes with medications, but I can't help you lose weight. You have to do that yourself."

The fear she'd known all her life knotted her muscles once again.

He wrote several prescriptions. "I don't know why you were burdened with this condition, Mattie. You may have fought the good battle, but the war goes ever on."

Her nails cut into her palm. "What if I don't lose weight?"

41

"It makes it that much harder to control other things -- more serious things. I urge you to consider it." He handed her several prescriptions. "You'll feel better."

Her sandals popped against her heels as she walked down the hall. Maybe she'd try one more time. The thought of being hungry depressed her. Maybe she'd start next week after Eddie's birthday.

He stood up as she came into the waiting room. "What did he say?"

She stuffed the prescriptions into her purse. "He says I'm fine."

"Good." He took her hand.

She took a deep breath. "Let's go get a pizza."

He kissed her fingers. "Pepperoni?"

She smiled. "That would be nice."

ELIZABETH ROSE

Summer – 1959

"What do you think, Jelly?" Elizabeth Rose sat behind the big two-toned steering wheel, trying to ignore the fiery knot in her stomach.

"It's one hell of a car, Miz Rose." Jelly Jenson wiped invisible fingerprints off the Dover White paint.

"I'm just a little old widow woman, counting on your advice." She peered into the rear view mirror. The fins of the 1959 Coup de Ville rose majestically behind her -- the chrome gleaming in the late afternoon glow. "It IS the best, isn't it?"

"Don't you worry, ma'am. It's one of a kind, just like you."

"Oh, Jelly." She smiled up at him. "How you do go on." She turned the key and the engine hummed.

He went out onto Church Street and held up traffic until she could maneuver the big car out of the parking lot. Waving at Jelly, she accelerated towards the setting sun.

The speedometer wavered around eighty as Elizabeth hit the straightaway just outside of town. She fumbled with the unfamiliar headlights as dusk melted into dark. There were no other cars, so she urged the Caddy on faster and faster -- the wind roaring in her ears. Just as she passed Plunkett's farm, she flipped on the radio. Someone was singing something about a sleeping lion.

The boy was walking along the side of the highway. She didn't see him until the last moment. Screaming, she swerved too late. The impact threw him over the top of the car. Spinning the wheel back to the right hard to stay on the road, she glanced in the rearview mirror in time to see the body bounce on the pavement. A thrill of fear went through her. What had she done? Braking, she twisted to squint into the darkness behind her. No one could survive that. What good would it do to stop? Besides, what's one nigger in the world more or less? She sped up.

In Simpson City, she pulled into a brightly lit drive-in and ordered a root beer float from a chubby waitress who skated up to her window in white shorts.

"Mighty nice car, ma'am."

Breathing heavily, Elizabeth took out her gold compact and dusted the shine off her nose. There was only the slightest trace of a quiver at the corner of her mouth.

"Biggest thing I ever saw." The carhop skated back towards the building.

Elizabeth blew air between her lips and clutched her midsection. After a moment, the spasm eased and she sat upright, tormented by an ugly thought. What if the kid had dented her new car? She got out and walked around the Caddy. There was a dark smudge on the chrome just under the double headlights on the right hand side. She used a lace handkerchief to wipe the spot. Blood! She stepped back in horror.

The root beer float didn't help her stomach. She left it melting on the tray hooked to her window. What if someone saw the accident? Her heart throbbed in her chest. No. That stretch of highway was almost a mile from niggertown. It wasn't likely anyone else was around to make trouble for her. She flashed her lights and the young woman skated out to take the tray.

44

As Elizabeth headed toward home, the radio was playing 'Cold, Cold Heart'. She turned it off.

• • • • •

The next morning dawned bright and crisp. A perfect day to take breakfast in the arbor, she thought as she sat on the edge of her bed rubbing her jaw. It was nice and shady out there. She might be fifty-two years old but she looked a good ten years younger when the sun wasn't in her face.

"Vonnie, make me a bowl of oatmeal," she said as she came into the kitchen.

"Yes, ma'am." Vonnie stood in front of the stove, crying, her pregnant belly trembling like Jello.

"Whatever's the matter, dear?" Elizabeth couldn't remember ever seeing Vonnie upset. The girl turned towards her with a puss only a darky could muster -- eyes swollen almost shut and her lips quivering.

"My little brother got killed last night."

"OH? What did he do?" Young nigger boys were always getting in trouble. It was their nature.

"He didn't do nothing, ma'am. He was walking along the highway around dusk. They think he was hit by something big -- a truck or something. He never had a chance."

Elizabeth felt twinges of last night's stomachache start again just below her breastbone. "How old was he?"

"He was only fourteen, ma'am." Vonnie wiped her eyes with the hem of her apron.

Elizabeth couldn't stand looking at the silly girl. "Well, he's gone now and there's nothing you can do about it. The way to get through this is to stay busy. Why don't you plan on defrosting the freezer and cleaning the oven before you leave today?"

Vonnie's eyes reflected something dark and ominous.

45

The little bitch! How dare Vonnie give her the evil eye? She was only trying to help her through her personal tragedy, after all. There was a time when a nigger wouldn't dare get snooty with a white woman.

Vonnie didn't go beyond the look. She just said 'Yes ma'am' and got to work on breakfast while Elizabeth went out on the patio to enjoy the cool autumn air.

"Aunt Betsy." Lexington Beland came around the corner of the house.

"My, my, don't you look nice." She lifted her cheek for his air-kiss.

"And you are the prettiest miniature rose in the garden." Lexington was her oldest sister's boy. Still a bachelor at thirty-five, he already had a bald spot on the back of his head. She knew he only came to see her because he wanted her money. That was fine with her. She'd been dangling the will over his head for years.

"What are you doing out here this time of the morning, Lexington?" She sipped her coffee, holding it in her mouth for a moment. The heat felt good on her aching jaw.

"I heard you got yourself a Coup De Ville, Auntie."

"Most elegant vehicle you've ever seen." Elizabeth took another sip.

"You gonna show it to me?"

"I'd like to eat my breakfast, first."

"Think I'll have Vonnie make me some eggs then." He sat down in the patio chair across the glass table from her, a thin cigar clenched in his teeth. "VONNIE, OH VONNIE, DARLIN."

"Yes sir, Mr. Beland." Vonnie waddled to the door with Elizabeth's breakfast. The oatmeal was thick and hot with a large chunk of butter -- not margarine -- and a scoop of brown sugar.

"Thank you, Vonnie." Elizabeth draped the napkin across her lap.

"Think you could fix me a mess of your Eggs Benedict, girlie?" Lexington's voice dripped honey. Hardly the way one should speak to a darky. Elizabeth telegraphed her disapproval with a glare.

"You want orange juice, too?"

"Orange juice and some of your good coffee with thick cream."

"Yes sir." Vonnie let the screen door slam behind her.

"Vonnie is in a bad mood," Lexington commented. "Problems with the baby?"

"Her brother got killed last night."

"Oh God. Damon? I'm sorry to hear that. He is -- was a fine young man."

"She's taking it out on me."

"Why is she taking it out on you?"

"Who knows why any of these people do what they do?" Elizabeth dipped her spoon into the oatmeal. "I'd just as soon not talk about it if you don't mind."

Lexington's eyes drifted to the back door.

"It's not the end of the world. You needn't look so troubled." Elizabeth laid down the spoon. Suddenly, she didn't have the energy to eat.

His sigh was long suffering. "So tell me about this De Ville of yours, Aunt Betsy. What possessed you to buy one?"

"Why shouldn't I have something nice?"

"It's a big car for a little lady like you. These things are like gold. Not too many being made."

"All the more reason for having one."

Vonnie brought Lexington his breakfast. "Auntie just told me about Damon, Vonnie."

"Yes, sir." She sniffed.

"I'm so very sorry."

Vonnie dropped the silverware on the table and waddled into the house, bawling.

Elizabeth had had her fill of that girl. Turning up pregnant without a husband was embarrassing enough. Now this!

Lexington stood up. "Vonnie!"

"She's fine. Sit down." Elizabeth rolled her eyes. "You can't go chasing after the hired help. It's not appropriate."

He glanced from Elizabeth to the door and back to Elizabeth.

"SIT DOWN, LEXINGTON."

"As you wish, Aunt Betsy." He bowed grandly.

"Don't be arrogant."

He sat down and dug into his breakfast.

"Don't chew with your mouth open."

"Okay, all done." He washed it down with his coffee. "Let's go check out the De Ville."

"You are going to have to do something about your table manners." She folded her napkin and laid it on the table. She turned to Vonnie who was waiting to clear. "Don't just stand there. Go get my purse."

• • • • •

Elizabeth and Lexington strolled arm in arm down the long curving drive to the coach house where she kept her cars.

"You are a cold-hearted bitch, Auntie."

She patted his hand playfully. "You don't want my money anymore?"

"Oh I want it -- just not enough to keep kissing your ass."
He grinned, his cigar clenched between his teeth.

"Your language, Lexington!"

"Try to put yourself in Vonnie's shoes. That's all I ask."

"How can I do that? It's not that I bear her any ill will, but
we are different at the core. My great grandfather owned a
plantation and a hundred darkies. Her great grandfather was a
slave. I am a lady. She's a maid. I'm white and she's as black as
the ace of spades."

"Yes, yes -- we are different. I know it's our heritage -- but
can't you be kind?"

"It says in the Bible plain as day --."

"You can make that book say anything you want, Aunt
Betsy. What if you are wrong?"

"What do you mean wrong?"

"What if this isn't how God wants people to live?"

"Of course, it's what He wants. Where do you get these
crazy ideas?"

"What if you misread the bible? What if the bible isn't what
everyone thinks it is? What then?"

"Don't be silly. It's the word of God. Ask anyone. Ask
Reverend Toole."

"What if we were meant to figure things out for ourselves,
Auntie? Wouldn't the rules be different then?"

She paused for a moment in front of the stable. "No matter
how you figure it, Lexington -- black is black and white is
white."

"Doesn't it strike you as odd that God made all these
people and then sends them to hell for not being Christian?"

She shook her head. "You are the strangest boy. You
always were. It's too much for ordinary folk to figure out.
That's why we follow the good book -- and it says that

everyone has to be born again or you can't enter the kingdom of God. I don't make the rules, for heaven's sake."

His eyes seemed sad to her. "I hoped that you'd soften up a little. Maybe bend a few of those rules?"

"Don't be ridiculous, Lexington. What good's a rule if you don't follow it?" She slipped a key into the padlock and he helped her pull back the heavy oaken door. The morning sun glinted off the Caddy's windshield.

"Wow! That baby's gotta be twenty foot long." He ran his hand over the hood.

"Nineteen," she corrected him.

"What's this?" He pointed to a rusty-red spot on the front fender.

"Nothing." Her stomach rolled. "Bird poop."

"Will you let me drive it?"

"Not in this life." She got in the car. "Get in and I'll give you a ride."

"I think I'll stay here for a while if you don't mind."

"Keep an eye on Vonnie. She probably thinks losing her brother is an excuse to be lazy." She waved him out of the way and eased the Caddy out of the garage.

• • • • •

She was passing Jelly Jenson's showroom when the pain hit her. Gasping for breath, she realized her heart wasn't beating anymore. The traffic sounds faded. The Coup de Ville coasted to a stop in the middle of the intersection just past Church Street.

"Miz Rose." Jelly Jenson threw open the door. His eyes were wide, the pupils dilated with alarm. "Are you okay? Something wrong with the car?"

She tried to answer but no words came.

"Miz Rose?"

Everything faded -- even the pain. She felt herself moving toward Jelly's eyes and into them and through them. Suddenly, she was in a vortex, being sucked upwards. She looked down and saw the Caddy. The roof was transparent and she saw Jelly Jenson shaking a tiny, red-haired woman. "That's ME!" Her eyes bulged and she stretched her hands back toward earth. "NO. I DON'T WANT TO GO."

There was a loud pop and she realized she'd broken through the membrane between life and death. It was too late. There was no going back, so she looked up. A dark cloud shimmered above her and she felt a warm and loving presence.

"It's you," she whispered.

"Yes."

"Is this it?"

"It is."

She relaxed and opened her arms. "I'm ready."

"Not yet."

She felt a rush of disappointment. "Why?"

"Don't you know?"

Scenes from her life flashed before her eyes in quick succession. Lying in her mother's arms. Falling off her bicycle. Playing with her sister. Going to school. Reading the Bible. Meeting Martin Rose. Loving him. Marrying him. Losing the first baby -- and the second one. Losing her sister. Losing Martin. Buying the Caddy.

"The boy! The nigger boy!"

Silence.

"That was an accident. I never meant to hit him."

Silence

"Then why?"

"Don't you know?"

She searched her heart. "I'm a good person. I followed the rules. I accepted Jesus."

"It's not enough."

"I don't understand."

"Come back when you do."

The words were like a palm in the face. She somersaulted backwards in space. The Caddy gleamed below her, the back doors thrown wide open -- the headlights illuminating the intersection. It was no longer a bright sunny fall morning, but a cold winter's night. Flashing lights in the distance. The police? No, an ambulance rushing toward the Coup de Ville where it sat on Church Street.

As she drifted downwards, she saw through the car's transparent roof. A dark skinned woman lay on the backseat, her dress up around her waist, her bare legs bent at the knees. A chunky man with a bald spot knelt between her thighs. The rushing sound of the wind grew louder and she swirled down and around into darkness.

Pressure. On all sides -- and a throbbing, pulsing beat. Above her and all around. Bubump. Bubump. Bubump. She was warm and wet and safe. Peaceful. She wanted to sleep, curled up in this perfect peaceful place -- but there was no time. In the distance was a pinprick of light.

The walls pressed in around her and she felt herself sliding toward the light. Bubump. Bubump. Bubump. It was faster now, louder. Something soft pressed against the top of her head. The light was bigger, closer. She was in a pool of warm water that was slowly draining away. Something opened and her head popped through another membrane into the cool night air. She opened her eyes. Tried to breathe.

She heard a familiar voice.

"There's the head. Come on, Vonnie. PUSH. You can do it."

She was turning. The walls pressed against her body and she squirted out onto the white leather upholstery of the Coup de Ville.

"It's a girl. Vonnie, it's a beautiful little girl."

"Is she okay?"

Big hands picked her up and wiped her face with a bit of cloth torn from her mother's skirt. "Come on now, little one." Lexington patted her on the back. "Breathe for me now. Breathe for Daddy."

She took a great breath and screamed.

"She's cold. Give her to me." Vonnie held out her arms.

"The ambulance will be here in a minute, my love. Jelly's bringing more blankets," Lexington said as he handed his new daughter to her mother.

"She's beautiful." The woman cradled her.

"I know this is a lot to ask, Vonnie, but I want to name her after Auntie, if that's okay with you."

Elizabeth Rose screamed, jerking her tiny brown arms and legs spasmodically. Was this hell? Or heaven?

Vonnie opened her blouse. Bubump, bubump, bubump. Elizabeth felt her mother's heart throbbing, soothing, warming her. Rooting, she found the great, dark nipple and suckled.

IN MY FASHION

I could see Synara inside Gino's. She was alone in the corner booth, focused on her book. All I had to do was walk in and sit down across from her. I knew she'd be glad to see me. I touched the glass. One push and the door would swing open. My palms were damp. She might look up at any moment. What would I say to her? I backed away and went to my car.

It was cold and my breath fogged the windows. I almost missed her when she came out and got into her shiny red Beemer. I waited until her taillights came on before starting my car. It was a short drive to her house. I parked down the block and strolled past her driveway just as the garage door closed. A heartbeat later the lights went on in the kitchen and I knew she was safe.

At home in my shower, I remembered how she smelled -- the soft sounds she made when I touched her, the electric charge between her soul and mine. She was a splash of color in a barren gray winter. Remembering her kept me sane.

I toweled off and examined the sores on my lips and gums. I took a swig of medicated mouthwash and sloshed it from cheek to cheek. All that did was replace one bad taste with another one. Pulling on a fleece-lined sweat suit, I shuffled into the kitchen and crushed the pills into a fine powder. Fruit flies buzzed around an over-ripe banana on the counter. I peeled it and mashed it with a fork. Mixing the drug with the sweet gooey mess made it easier to swallow.

Sitting in my recliner, I cradled my laptop computer and logged onto the Internet. Synara was online -- most likely working on her novel. I scanned the headlines, waiting for her to notice me. "No Cure for Mysterious Disease" caught my attention. Big news! I'd long given up hope.

"It's been six months since I saw Eric." The familiar bell alerted him to her message. "I'm worried about him."

"I'm sure he's fine."

"I hope so."

"He's a son of a bitch, leaving you like that." I sipped some herbal tea to keep my mouth moist. "Forget him and move on."

"This one was different, Herbie."

"Why?"

"I recognized him -- a creative mind, a generous spirit -- I don't know, exactly. He touched me, I guess."

I swallowed back tears. Let go, let go, let go! "He's a jerk." I paused before sending the message. Was I going too far? No, I no longer believe in miracles. I hit enter.

"Eric would never hurt me."

"How can you go on believing in him?"

"I'm like that -- besides, he deserves my faithfulness."

"My God, Synara. You never got that far. How can you be faithful to a man you never slept with?"

"Fidelity isn't about sex."

I sat quietly, thinking about how much I wanted her in every way. "What is it then?"

"It's about being there when he needs me, watching his back -- caring about him, never bad-mouthing him."

"It should go both ways." My heart was breaking.

"I can't explain it, but I think it does."

"After six months of silence?"

"I feel him, Herbie. It's the strangest thing. I KNOW he's around. I know he loves me."

"You're crazy."

"I suppose I am."

I held my breath. "What happens if you never see him again?"

"I'll go on loving him, I guess."

"He's a lucky man."

"I think I'm the lucky one."

I held my hand to the screen, trying to absorb her essence. "How?"

"I wake up every day wishing him well, wanting good things for him. When it's sunny, I imagine him outside enjoying the taste of the breeze. When it rains, I think about him snuggled up in bed with a good book. Knowing he's in the world makes me notice everything more. It's an incredible gift -- Eric's existence."

I shifted in my seat, the pain in my gut dulled by the drugs -- but not quelled. "You're a romantic."

"Am I? I never thought of it that way."

"So what's the gist here? You are going to wait for him?"

"Of course not. I don't need him, Herbie. I love him. My life will go on. It already has. After all, that's how I met you."

Guilt bubbled in my stomach like a greasy stew. "This is hardly the same thing."

"Is it any less real?"

As my illness progressed, I couldn't endure reality. Even cloaked in anonymity, I needed her to think I was healthy and virile. Her not knowing made it easier to face a darkening screen.

"Herbie? Are you there?"

Gasping for air, I typed with one hand. "I'm here."

"Are you okay?"

"Fine."

"Want to talk to someone else?"

"NO!"

"What's wrong?"

"Hard day. I tried to be something I'm not and it got to be too much."

"Let go and be yourself."

It was hard to type. "I don't have a choice anymore."

"Herbie?"

"What?"

"Want to see some pretty pictures?"

"Yes."

She sent me a link. I struggled to click on it.

"This was me and Eric at our favorite restaurant. I was there tonight and I could have sworn I saw him out on the sidewalk looking in."

I knew she was special that first night at Gino's -- I promised her my heart right then and there.

"Here we are at the lake."

I stared at the picture of us splashing in the water. It was summer -- the last time we'd been together. I wanted to say thank you, but it was too late. The lights flickered. I couldn't hold on any longer. I hoped I hadn't hurt her too much. Letting go was my last gift -- the only way I knew how to love her.

The Brafferton

Gettysburg, Pennsylvania – 2004

Get interested in someone else's war, the doctor had advised. It'll put things in perspective. It'll get you talking. The doctor had it all wrong. Living history wasn't going to help. Kirby parked in the city lot on Stratton Street across from St. James Church and headed back to The Brafferton. He'd enjoyed wandering around the Gettysburg reenactment site with his wife. He hadn't even minded standing outside the Sutler's tents while she bought feathered bonnets and wide petticoats. All the muskets and sabers hadn't bothered him either -- but it was a different story when the cannonade began. Choking back panic, he'd pleaded a headache and left Peg to watch Pickett's Charge with friends.

The traffic light changed as he approached York Street. A young woman in a yellow Honda stopped. Kirby nodded to her before stepping off the curb. He was halfway across the intersection when he heard an engine revving. He whirled as a large truck crashed into the rear of the little car sending it straight toward him.

He locked eyes with the driver. Her mouth was open. When he couldn't stand it anymore, he jumped to the right. The Honda crashed into a pole a few feet away. The woman's head smashed through the windshield and then the truck crushed her little car. Yellow splashed with red and gray was the last thing he saw.

• • • • •

58

The air conditioner was running full blast. Kirby rolled over onto his back, smacking his lips. Something crusty caked the corner of his mouth. Where was he? He sat up and looked around. The minie ball in the mantle, the slipper bench at the foot of the big cherry bedstead, the armoire -- somehow he was back in his room at The Brafferton.

Throwing back the comforter, he staggered into the bathroom to stare at his reflection in the mirror over the sink. Nothing was broken -- just a cut inside his swollen lower lip. He took a shuddering breath. It made no sense. He was nearing eighty years old yet he was unharmed and the young woman was -- he closed his eyes trying to force his mind to go blank.

It didn't work any more. He bent over the sink and splashed cool water on his face. The images flickered behind his eyes like an old time movie -- big ships bombarding the tiny island, climbing into the rocking Higgins boat, dead bodies scattered on the black beach. A yellow scarf fluttering -- NO!

Dabbing a wet washcloth at the dried blood in the corner of his mouth, Kirby froze as he reentered the bedroom. A stranger in a gray uniform stood by the window peering over the air conditioner down into the street.

"Who the hell are you?"

The figure didn't move. "They can't get her out," he said.

The man seemed at home. Most everyone in Gettysburg dressed in costume during reenactments. Maybe he worked at the inn and had come to the front room on the second floor to watch the excitement -- just another ghoul.

Kirby picked up his wife's roller bag and laid it on the bed. "They can take their time. She's not going to make it."

"Damnation." The man shuddered but kept his eyes on the spectacle in the street. "You ever notice when something happens like that -- something gruesome -- that it's hard to look away even though you want to?"

Kirby had spent a lifetime trying not to look. "How did I get up here?"

"The innkeeper. You were upset. Don't you remember?"

"Vaguely."

A loud crash outside and they both flinched.

"Jaws of life."

The soldier seemed confused. "What?"

"They are tearing the car apart to get to her." Kirby unzipped the side pocket of the bag and stuck his hand inside. Where the hell did Peg pack that baggie?

The sound of screeching metal rose from the street. They eyed each other nervously. Kirby dumped the contents of Peg's bag onto the bed. The soldier watched Kirby sort through the objects on the comforter. "I always did like this room," he said. "Of course, it was a bit different when first I visited."

There it was! Kirby pocketed Peg's bottle of pills. "When was that?"

"Evening of the first day. We got here around three o'clock and pushed the Federals back through town -- killing some, capturing others. I slipped away and wandered through the butcher shop next door. Others had been there before me but I found a scrap of ham they missed and put it in my pocket."

Another performer. Kirby groaned. "Save it until my wife comes back from the reenactment. I'm not in the mood for a performance."

"The family that lived here was gone -- hiding somewhere I guess. They left the front door open. I climbed the stairs. Children's things -- toys, clothes, books -- filled this room. The bed was rumpled as if someone had been napping only a few minutes before. When I bent over to touch the coverlet, some Yankee shot at me. Came through that window right there. Zipped over my head and hit the mantle. If I'd been standing it would have hit me between the eyes."

"ENOUGH!" Kirby threw Peg's hairbrush across the room. It hit the armoire and clattered to the floor. Unperturbed, the Confederate soldier turned to look out the window again.

"Do I have to call the innkeeper?"

"It wouldn't make any difference."

The man's equanimity puzzled Kirby. Did the innkeeper hire this wacko to keep an eye on him until they found Peg? Was he hurt worse than he thought? "What's your name?"

"Private Jack Daily. Seventh Louisiana Infantry. Hays' Brigade."

More Civil War nonsense. "Mr. Daily, I'm not feeling well. I'd like you to leave now." Kirby marched across the room. Reaching for Jack's elbow to escort him to the door, he gasped as his hand went through the soldier's arm. Kirby drew back and rubbed his chilled fingers. "What are you," he whispered.

"You HAD to do that, didn't you?" Jack brushed invisible wrinkles from his sleeve. "I was standing here not bothering anyone and you get all worked up and go after me."

"What do you want of me?" Kirby could hardly get the words out.

"I don't want anything. I was here first."

Kirby had never heard of any ghosts at The Brafferton, but old places like this soaked up sorrowful experiences like a bloody sponge. Did the inn have painful memories too? "Why do I see you?"

Jack returned his gaze to the accident scene. "I don't know exactly. Most folks don't."

Already losing his fear, Kirby peeked out the window too. Emergency vehicles and firemen filled the intersection. They were lifting the woman's body out of the wreckage. "Why her? If the light had changed ten seconds sooner she'd be safe now."

"I don't rightly know." Jack stood at attention while the attendants arranged the body on a gurney and covered it with a sheet.

"It's so arbitrary." Kirby swallowed back tears.

"Aye."

The trucker who'd caused the accident hovered near the wreckage, wringing his hands. "Look at that poor bastard." Kirby wiped the corner of his eye with his knuckle. "One stupid mistake and he kills someone."

"Welcome to hell, brother," Jack said through clenched teeth.

Kirby focused on the gurney sliding into the back of the ambulance and touched the bottle of Valium in his pocket. "You made the trip to the other side?"

"Aye."

"You know how things are?"

Jack shrugged. "I know about how. I'm short on why."

A sudden thought struck Kirby. "I'm not already dead am I?"

Jack snorted. "Do you feel dead?"

Kirby touched the glass over the air conditioner, leaving a fingerprint. Disappointed, he frowned. "No."

"Don't rush it, my friend. It doesn't solve anything."

"I just want peace."

The ghost laughed again. "What do you expect? Cherubs and harps? Paradise? You are still you on this side of the veil."

"Then what's the point?" Kirby had counted on things being okay once he passed on. No more guilt. No more sorrow. No more nightmares. A clean slate.

"There is no point." Jack took off his hat and held it over his heart. The trucker stood in the middle of York Street watching the ambulance bearing the young woman's body drive away. "You move on. It's as simple as that."

The room was icy cold. Kirby hugged himself, trying not to think about the crushing burden of culpability that never went away no matter how sorry you were.

A policeman took the trucker's arm and led him to a squad car parked in front of the church.

"What are you looking for, my friend?" Jack fixed Kirby through the corner of his eye. "Absolution?"

Kirby was taken aback. "I'd hoped -- that's what they preach anyway."

"Doesn't that strike you as immoral? Shuffling off your debts onto some other innocent soul?"

Kirby had to admit he thought the preacher's version of redemption seemed too easy. "I guess I was being unrealistic."

Jack returned his gaze to the accident scene. "You have a bad case of soldier's heart."

Such quaint terms for the devastation of war -- soldier's heart, shell shock, battle fatigue. It went on and on -- generation after generation. How could the doctor think that the suffering of others would somehow ease Kirby's personal nightmare?

Jack craned his neck. The trucker was trying to explain -- pointing down York Street, then at the wreckage in the intersection. "We'd be monsters if what we did didn't bother us."

Kirby leaned his forehead against the window. "Maybe we are monsters for doing what we did in the first place."

"I was a boy when I went to war." Jack shifted his musket to the other shoulder and moved so he could view the street from another angle. "My brother and I were going to be heroes. We were fighting against tyranny and for freedom. People would look up to us and thank us for our service. It seemed right and moral at the time."

The policeman took a notepad out of his pocket -- scribbled something -- asked a question. The trucker slumped his shoulders and shook his head.

Kirby understood the trucker's instinct to deny responsibility. It was natural. A moment of carelessness -- or irrational fear -- or anger could have such awful consequences. He squeezed his eyes shut. "I volunteered for the Marines in 1944 with my best friends -- Jimmy O'Rourke and Billy Benson. I was engaged to Billy's little sister at the time. There was a party at the firehouse to send us off. I felt ten feet tall. It was the last time I can remember being truly happy with myself."

Jack turned away from the window and backed into the corner. "I didn't think about dying. That was something that happened to other guys. I thought about killing though." He sighed. "I was a fool."

The policeman slipped the notebook into his back pocket and pointed to the squad car. The trucker turned around and put his hands on the roof of the cruiser. The cop patted his sides, feeling his pockets. Handcuffing the man's hands behind him, he put him in the vehicle and drove away. Another policeman set out yellow traffic cones and began directing cars around the accident site.

"The Japs attacked us. We were going to kick their butts all the way back across the Pacific Ocean." The movie in Kirby's head sped up -- the mad race across the beach and up the slope in knee deep sand, the massive explosion that threw him on his back, the bits of brain and bone that clung to his body. Memories he'd avoided for over sixty years washed over him. Oblivion was better. He reached for the pills in his pocket.

Jack bowed his head. "When I left my post that day, I was running away. I came here -- to this room -- to die."

Shocked by Jack's words, Kirby fumbled the medicine bottle. The cap came off and yellow pills rolled across the rug. How many old soldiers found their way to The Brafferton, he wondered. How many troubled souls had taken refuge in this room?

"Gettysburg was chaotic. The wounded from both sides lay moaning in the streets. My brother and I chased a bluecoat through the Diamond. Near High Street, a cannonball blew Daniel's leg off. He bled to death in minutes crying for our mother. As he paled and left me in a pool of gore, I saw the Federal we'd been chasing head back toward York. I lost my head and went after the bastard." Jack's voice trembled. "Just as he reached that intersection right out there, I sent the bastard to hell with a musket ball through the head."

A tow truck arrived to retrieve what was left of the yellow Honda. "Justice," Kirby muttered as he watched a second one drive away with the wrecked truck. "Did that make you feel better?"

"Aye. At first it felt damn good. I ran up and kicked the son of a bitch in the ribs. That's for my baby brother, I yelled. That's for Daniel. My shot destroyed most of the face, but I knew he was young because he had no facial hair whatever -- not even peach fuzz. I stripped off his tunic looking for ammunition. It was then I saw that this wasn't a boy but a woman. She'd stuffed a pistol in the front of her trousers. When I removed it, I was shocked to realize that she was with child. I backed away. There were people in the church taking care of the wounded but I couldn't face them -- or anyone. I turned toward the Diamond. Bleeding soldiers limped my way leaning on their muskets. Dazed, I ducked into the butcher shop and then into this house."

"You'd just lost your brother. She was dressed like the enemy -- how were you to know?"

"It was quiet up here. The toys made me think of Daniel when we were boys. I remembered the fear in my mother's eyes when we left home. She told us to take care of each other. The numbness gave way to pain. I couldn't go home without my brother. I'd rather lie down on the bed with the woman's pistol under my chin than tell our mother Daniel was dead."

"One quick pull on the trigger," Kirby said dreamily.

"I lay there thinking about Daniel and the girl and her baby and the minie ball that just missed me. The bed was soft and a warm breeze came in through the broken window. I heard voices in the street. After awhile, my arm got tired and I let the pistol drop onto the bed. I remembered the scrap of ham in my pocket and stuffed it in my mouth. As I chewed, I looked around the room. After a bit I got up and went back out into the street."

"What made you stop?"

"The ham was greasy."

"Greasy?"

"And my canteen was empty."

"You didn't kill yourself because you were thirsty?"

"No. I didn't kill myself because when I went to find water, I saw her body lying in the street."

A loud screech from the street startled Kirby. The workers hooked the crumpled yellow car to the tow truck and pulled it away from the post.

Kirby's breathing escalated -- short quick inhalations as the flashback swept over him. There was no escaping the smell. It clung to him like sticky black molasses. Big black beetles crawled over the corpses. Kirby flicked one off Jimmy O'Rourke's stiff hand. Scuffling footsteps in the distance. Kirby cowered behind the pile of bodies until he couldn't stand it anymore. Jumping to his feet, he fired into the darkness until there were no more bullets in his rifle. "Die, you yellow bastard," he shouted before dropping behind the rotting remains of his friends.

"I couldn't leave her there," Jack continued. "And I had to go take care of Daniel."

At dawn, Kirby peeked over the pile of bodies. Something yellow fluttered in the distance. Kirby looked left and right before crawling out to investigate.

66

"I carried the girl to the church over there although I knew she was dead." Jack pointed out the window. "I figured someone would take care of her eventually."

Kirby sucked in air faster and faster.

"Then I went looking for Daniel. I ran back to where his blood stained High Street. He was gone. I raced through Gettysburg -- checking the houses and barns and stables and stores -- turning over bodies lying on the streets and on stretchers outside the hospitals."

Kirby slithered across the rocky ground on his belly zeroing in on the flash of color. As he got closer, he saw a dead Marine lying on his side. The man had tied a yellow scarf around his bloody arm. SHIT! SHIT! SHIT! Kirby pounded the earth with his fists. He'd killed another American.

"I wandered throughout the town looking for Daniel all night and most of the next day. In the afternoon, the guns started again. I knew I should go back to my unit but I couldn't until I found Daniel. I came back and hid in this room -- standing guard at this window, watching that church in case someone brought in my brother's body."

Kirby rolled the Marine over. His eyes bulged. It was Billy Benson. Peg's big brother -- his last remaining friend from home. He must have screamed but he couldn't remember hearing it. "I'm sorry, I'm sorry!" The tourniquet was too loose. Maybe if he tightened it, Billy would have a chance. Sure. That's all he needed. Then he'd be fine. He retied the yellow scarf on the dead boy's arm. There now. That's better. Sliding his hands under Billy's armpits, he pulled him back toward the wall of corpses. "Let's get out of here before a sniper sees us." He was halfway across the clearing when he saw the gut wound.

"I hid here on the third day too. The war went on without me. I went home to face mother's sorrow -- and my own. I lived another seventy years looking for Daniel." The ghost turned back toward the church. "I'm still looking for him."

"They pinned us down, you see -- and they all died -- everyone but me." It was impossible for anyone who wasn't there to understand. That knowledge had kept Kirby mute since 1945. How could he tell Peg about Billy? How could he tell anyone?

A road worker swept up the glittering pieces of glass in the road below them. "They are clearing away the last of the wreckage," Jack reported.

Kirby sighed. So now he knew why he felt rotten -- why he had nightmares, why loud noises made him flinch. What good was that? It didn't change things. Billy wasn't coming back -- nor Jimmy O'Rourke or Daniel Daily or the pregnant woman Jack killed or the girl in the yellow Honda.

"Here comes the innkeeper with your wife," Jack said softly.

"I better get these pills back into Peg's bag."

The front door opened. "He's upstairs." Kirby heard the innkeeper say.

"I'm coming, Kirby darling." Peg sounded out of breath.

Kirby stuffed the pill bottle under the cushion and sat down in the high backed chair, bracing himself to face Peg. "Are you still there?" He whispered over his shoulder to the ghost.

"Aye. We all are."

JUST HOLD ME

1967

The lake quivered in the moonlight like black Jello. He parked under a willow tree and fiddled with the radio. Soft rock and roll music filled the car. "You like the Animals?"

She nodded, her odd green eyes looking through him like superman's x-ray vision.

He fished half of a joint out of his pocket and lit it. Filling his lungs, he closed his eyes and held his breath. "Yeah. The Animals are cool." The words gushed out of his mouth along with the smoke.

She rolled down the window.

He held up the joint. "Does this bother you?"

She shook her head.

He didn't really care if it did. In fact, he hoped it shocked the hell out of her. "Want a hit?"

"No, that's all right."

Good. He didn't want to share it anyway. Two more drags and he put it out, carefully saving the butt. He'd need it later -- when he went home.

"Why did you bring me here, Gary?"

"I wanted to get to know you." It wasn't really a lie. Well, sort of a lie. "I couldn't stand being with all those people, but I didn't want to be alone."

She didn't flinch. "I understand that."

"You do?"

She nodded. "All that craziness -- it's okay sometimes, but it didn't seem right tonight."

He snorted. "You got that right." What had he been thinking coming back to campus? It had only been two years since he flunked out but everything was different now. The students were still his age, but they seemed cleaner than he remembered -- shinier.

"I'm sorry about Donna," she said.

"Yeah, well. I should have called."

"Didn't she write you?"

He slammed his fist against the steering wheel. "Not that she was going off to have some damned hippy's baby she didn't." Of course, it had been months since she'd written at all. He'd told himself that when he got back to the states there would be a big pile of letters waiting for him. It was stupid, but you tell yourself all kinds of things when you're humping through the jungle.

The girl lowered her eyes. "I don't know what to say."

"Well, Betty -- that is your name, isn't it?"

"Bonnie."

"Not much you can say, now is there, Bonnie? It's the old out of sight out of mind story."

"Things happen, Gary. It's not like you were married -- or even engaged."

"Don't I have a right to expect things to be the same after what I've done? For her? For you?"

Her eyebrows rose. "Me?"

"You know what I mean. For the country. For the good old US of A."

"I never asked you to go off to war."

"Well, someone sure as hell did."

"It wasn't me." She turned away to stare out the window.

The growing distance between them infuriated him and he wanted to hurt her. "I came back to see Donna -- not some skinny consolation prize."

"Fine." She opened the door.

"What the hell are you doing?" He grabbed her arm before she could get out.

"Leaving."

His heart pounded. "It's ten miles back to the dorm."

"I know the way." She jerked her arm away.

"Come on, Bonnie. It's dark out there."

"What do you care?"

Funny thing was that he did care. She reminded him of his kid sister and he didn't want anything bad to happen to her. "I'm sorry. I was in hell day before yesterday. I'm not used to planet earth yet."

"Hell?" Those green eyes gave him the heebie-jeebies.

"Sure wasn't paradise." He tried to smile but it trembled on his lips. "Please stay with me, Bonnie."

She relaxed and closed the door. "I know you are disappointed about Donna, but there were any number of pretty girls at that party. I'm not exactly a cheerleader. Why did you pick me?"

Why DID he pick her? "You seem nice -- you're not a dog."

She blinked and he knew he'd said the wrong thing.

71

"You didn't look like you'd bite." He'd forgotten how to be nice long enough to get what he wanted. The rules were different in Nam.

"Aren't you glad to be home?" She laid her hand on his shoulder. It looked small and impossibly white on his uniform. It was the first time anyone had touched him in a long time.

"I am." His nose burned. "But you know, Nam sucks. It sucks so bad that I'm scared it'll suck me right back."

She leaned over to kiss him on the cheek. "It's over now, at least for you. You're home safe and sound, thank God."

"I'm alive." He wiped his nose with the back of his hand.

She shook his shoulder and smiled. "You're alive, Gary -- and in one piece."

"WHOOOOEEEE!" He clapped his hands and howled. "I made it back and I'm not dead or maimed."

The echoes of his voice faded and the silence grew between them again. She let go of his shoulder and leaned back in her seat. "Your folks must be relieved."

"They don't know I'm back yet."

She didn't say anything.

"I'm scared to go home." The admission filled the space between them.

"Why?"

He patted his pocket. The soft dreamy state he sought eluded him. Maybe another hit? No. He'd wait. The silence seemed loud, and he was aware of her eyes again. "What?"

"Why are you scared to go home?"

"Because it's not the same."

"Did they move or paint the house?"

"No."

"Then it's still the same. Maybe it's you that's changed."

She had him there. "I'm not ready to face my mother."

"She loves you."

"Yes." He never doubted his mother's love -- not once, but then how would she feel if she knew about Nam. Really knew?

"She's proud of you, Gary." Was she reading his mind?

"I know."

She pulled a tissue out of her purse and handed it to him. "Why does that upset you?"

"It doesn't." He blew his nose.

"You're their hero."

"I'M NOT A HERO!"

She shrank from him.

"I'm sorry." He was afraid she'd try to leave again. "I'm a crazy, bastard. Don't mind me."

"Why are you yelling at me?"

He thought of the months in Quang Ngai. "I'm not a hero."

"Okay."

He took a deep breath. Maybe this was a bad idea. "Do you want me to take you back?"

She looked at her watch. "Curfew is twelve thirty."

"What happens if you don't make it?"

"I always make it."

"Shit." He started the car.

"What's wrong, Gary?"

He turned to her, his jaw twitching. "I thought maybe you'd stay with me."

"You don't even know me."

That was the best part. "I need to be with someone."

"I'm not going to have sex with you."

"Ah, jeez," he groaned. "Did I ask for sex?"

"It's your first night back in the states. You should be with your family."

"I need to work up to it, okay?" He killed the engine and leaned his forehead against the steering wheel.

"Okay."

He wasn't sure what she meant. "Okay, what?"

"I'll stay with you."

"All night?"

"If I miss curfew, I might as well."

He was relieved, but now that she'd agreed he didn't know what to do next. "Should we get a motel room?"

"I don't think so." Her laugh softened the no.

"Maybe just stay here awhile and then go for breakfast?"

"What will we do all that time?"

It was a fair question. He wasn't sure he knew the answer though. "We can talk."

"You want to tell me about Nam?"

He shook his head -- then nodded slowly.

"We aren't going to be friends, are we?" She saw through him again.

"I hope we will be." It was a desperate lie.

"But we won't see each other after tonight, will we?"

He weighed his options. Would she change her mind if he answered honestly? "No," he said finally. "I don't think so."

"I see."

But she didn't. How could she? In truth, it didn't matter to him if she did or not. He gripped the steering wheel.

She stared out the window for a few moments. "Let's cut through the bullshit. What is it that you really want?"

His need made him brave. "I want you to hold me."

She stiffened.

"That's all. I promise I won't hurt you or anything."

"Just trust you?"

"You did that when you agreed to come out here with me." Why did he say that? She was probably thinking he was a rapist. He softened his voice. "I promise, Bonnie."

"Just hugs?"

He wet his lips. "Yeah."

She held out her arms and he slid across the front seat. Close up, her Ivory Soap scent was overwhelming. When he laid his head on her shoulder, her long shimmering hair brushed against his cheek. He snuggled closer and she wrapped her thin arms around him.

Her kindness overwhelmed him. "Oh my God," he murmured into her neck. "My God, my God, my God."

She stroked the back of his head. "Shush."

Outside the car, the wind rose and rustled the drooping willow branches. His sobs shook both of them. "I'm so scared."

"Everyone is, sweety." It was barely a whisper. He felt it rather than heard it.

"How can I go back to church?"

She rocked him in her arms. "You don't have to."

"Things got all mixed up over there."

"I know, I know."

He knew that she didn't have a clue what she was saying. She was a nineteen-year-old sophomore. What the hell did she know about war? But as long as she held him, he didn't care. "I hate what I did -- who I am."

"I don't hate you, Gary." She kissed his forehead.

It felt wonderful -- but of course, if she really knew him, she'd hate him too. They all would. His sister who looked up to him. His dad. His mother. How could anyone understand? He wasn't fit for ordinary life. Maybe he'd go off by himself -- be a hermit. No, he wasn't strong enough to go through life alone. Anguish overcame him and he moaned, "What am I going to do?"

She pulled back and put a hand on each cheek, holding his face inches from her own. "Leave it here. No one will ever know. Just leave it here."

"Yeah. That's it. I'll leave it here." It was a great idea. He'd push it all out of his thoughts. The old out of sight out of mind solution.

He curled back up in her arms and closed his eyes.

Lightning split the sky over the dark lake and big drops of rain splatted on the roof of the car. It reminded him of the rain in Nam -- and that reminded him of the flooded rice paddies -- and that reminded him of the people in their peaked straw hats bent over in the fields -- and that reminded him of the water buffalo -- and that reminded him of -- shit. He opened his eyes.

"I can't leave it here," he said.

She tried to move but he clung to her. "I don't have any answers, Gary. I'm a kid -- just like you. You are going to have to figure it out for yourself."

He stared at the raindrops beating against the windshield. She was right. It was foolish to think it would go away in one night. He had a lifetime to concentrate on forgetting. He shivered at the prospect.

"Are you okay?" She whispered.

"Just hold me."

LILITH

"We followed this asshole through the house and ended up in a little courtyard where we lost him. There are buildings on all four sides. It was like this guy disappeared into the fog." Mickey the Mountain bit into his cruller and chased it with hot black coffee.

"So where did he go?" Lamont leaned his elbows on the counter, his eyes wide and his bottom lip drooping.

"The sarge and I decide to split up. He goes to the left, checking doors and windows. I go to the right, flashlight in hand. It's downright spooky in there but hell, it'd take one crazy son of a gun to take me down so I'm not scared. Anyway, I hear this clanking sound as I get close to the far corner. I lower my gun and nearly squeeze off a shot when I see this little pooch chained outside of his dog house."

"You didn't hurt the doggie, did you?" Laverne gasped and covered her mouth.

Mickey brushed crumbs off the front of his uniform and polished a stray drop of coffee from his badge with a napkin. "Naw, I might look mean, little lady, but I'm as soft as angel food cake on the inside."

"Yeah, Mickey the Mountain wouldn't shoot a dog." Lamont looked askance at Laverne's exaggerated concern.

"So where was the bad guy?" Laverne refilled Mickey's cup.

"Inside the dog house."

"Naw! How did he get in there?" Lamont was aghast.

"Kicked that little puppy out of his warm cozy nest and crawled in himself. Me and the sarge tried to talk him out but now that he was inside, he couldn't move. We had to lift the roof off and help him stand up." Mickey picked up his second donut and winked at Laverne who giggled and blushed.

"HELP! HELP ME!" A tiny septuagenarian burst through the glass doors and ran to Mickey the Mountain. Clinging to the big cop's pant leg, he turned to look behind him -- his eyes bulging.

"Mr. Rubenstein, what is it?" Laverne hurried around the counter to take his arm while the glass doors slowly closed, the bell tinkling over the man's breathy pants.

"It's Lilith," he sobbed. "You've got to hide me."

"Let's put you in the kitchen, okay?" Laverne slipped her arm around Rubenstein's shoulders. Lamont helped her guide him through the chrome door while Mickey retrieved his baton and stepped out into the sidewalk, scanning the neighborhood for the threatening Lilith. Two little girls were jumping rope in front of the apartment building across the street. A black kid in high top tennis shoes and a satin jacket leaned against a tree with a boom box propped on one shoulder. An old woman sat on a bench in the park a half block away. A painting contractor dabbed pale pink onto the window trim of an old Victorian two doors down. Not seeing anything unusual, the cop put his stick away and went back inside the donut shop.

Rubenstein cowered in the far corner of the backroom with Laverne kneeling beside him and Lamont shuffling from one foot to the other, chewing his bottom lip.

"Lamont, will you and Laverne go on up front and take care of business?" Mickey stood with his legs apart, his hands on his hips staring down at the frightened old man while the two clerks returned to the front of the store.

The bald head was bowed, the swollen, arthritic fingers clasped around his knees.

"Are you okay, Jake?"

The old man looked up, his pale eyes locking onto Mickey's, and shook his head, his loose jowls quivering.

"You want to tell me what this is all about?"

"Don't let her find me. She'll kill me this time."

Mickey squatted down beside him. "Who's going to kill you?"

Jake leaned forward and cupped his hand over his lips. "Lilith!"

"Who is Lilith, Jake?"

"She's got the body of a whore and the heart of a devil."

"A what?"

Jake hadn't been himself since his triple by-pass three years back. He shuffled up and down Elm Street, his head bobbing between his shoulders -- his eyes cast down toward his feet. Once in a while, he tossed M&M's to the pigeons. Sometimes he banged on Mrs. Fry's picket fence with his cane just to aggravate the old biddy who came screaming out onto the porch with her cell phone in hand.

Mickey usually caught the call around lunchtime. He'd leave his sandwich half-eaten on the coffee shop counter and rush over to herd Jake back home before Mrs. Fry charged him with a can of bug spray or Jake walloped her upside the head with his cane. God forbid that he ever be on vacation when the two old enemies clashed.

"A succubus! A wraith with fiery eyes and long flowing hair the color of taffy." He drew her shape in the air with his hands. "She found me two days ago and kept me prisoner in my bed, having her way with me. At first I thought I was dreaming but it went on and on. I'm seventy-eight years old. After three or four times, I needed a rest -- but she continued licking and sucking on me until my blood pressure went through the roof. She's trying to kill me, I tell you."

"I love that dream, man. Wish I had it more often." Mickey chuckled and patted the frightened man on the shoulder. Jake had obviously run into one of the prostitutes on Bleeker Street four blocks away. The woman probably thought he had money. She was trying to get in the will and then wear the old man out. Death by sex. What a way to go. "Why don't you tell me where I can find this Lilith and I'll go talk to her about leaving you alone."

"You have to watch out for her, Officer. All she wants is sex. No kisses unless her tongue is down your throat. No caresses unless they are to arouse. She won't even talk to you afterwards. Doesn't want to snuggle. None of that. As soon as it's over, she starts right in again and if things stall -- if you know what I mean," Jake raised his eyebrows, "she scratches and bites. You should see my back."

Mickey laughed out loud. "No, that's okay. I don't need to see your battle scars. How did you get away from this wench?"

"I tricked her. Told her I had to have a Belgian Waffle or it wouldn't work at all. She backed away, her pointy tongue flickering between her lips -- her eyes scorching me as I got dressed. I'm sure she thought I was going to fuss with the toaster, but I escaped out the back door. I even left my cane behind. When I was half way down the block, she howled like a banshee and it chilled my bones. I'm what she wants and she won't rest until she's found me."

"Yeah, you are quite the stud, but don't you think she'll move on if she doesn't see you around?"

"You don't know Lilith. No one can refuse her." The front door bell rang and Jake cringed. "It's her! She's found me."

"Now you just hold on. I'll go out and see who's there. If it's this Lilith I'll send her on her way." Mickey stood up and peered through the window in the kitchen door. "It's only Mrs. Fry."

"Don't tell her I'm here." Jake covered his face with his hands.

"Why do you and Mrs. Fry have such a hard time getting along, Jake?"

"She has the heart of a whore and the eyes of a hawk."

None of it made sense to Mickey. "You stay put. I'll go speak with her."

Mrs. Fry sat at the counter with a maple donut and a latte when Mickey returned to the serving area. "Howdy Do, Mickey." Her false teeth clicked when she spoke. "Laverne was telling me about that madman Jake Rubenstein."

"Now I don't want any trouble. There are enough problems out there without me having to run interference between the two of you." Mickey tapped the counter to emphasize his point.

"I'm having my donut, not bothering a soul." Felicia Fry batted her fake eyelashes at Mickey the Mountain.

"Keep it that way." Mickey tossed two dollars down on the counter. "Keep the change, Lamont."

"What do you want us to do with -- oops!" Lamont clapped a hand over his mouth, but jerked his eyes toward the kitchen.

Mickey sighed. "Let him be. He'll come out when he feels like it." He shook his finger at Mrs. Fry. "I mean it, lady. You finish up your snack and go on home."

"I'm fresh out of Raid today." She sucked the sugar off each of her fingers, her eyes on Mickey's lips.

"And cut that out. It's not going to do you any good. I'm married with six kids." The old whore came on to every male in the neighborhood but you'd have to be pretty hard up to let Felicia Fry lure you into her web.

"So who's asking you for a date?" Her polyester wig was askew and lipstick ran into the dozens of small lines emanating from her mouth.

"I'm your man, Miz Fry." Lamont pumped his pelvis. "I'll be your boy toy."

Laverne giggled.

"Okay, okay. Cut it out, all of you. I need to know if you know who this Lilith is. Jake's description is a little flaky -- I'm guessing brown and blonde. Tall. At least taller than Jake. Long hair."

"Doesn't take a tall woman to outstretch that pipsqueak." Mrs. Fry sipped her coffee.

"I never heard tell of anyone like that around here, Mickey. Maybe she's a stranger? Maybe she followed Jake home from McDonald's?" Laverne's eyes were worried.

"Could be. What about you, Lamont? Anything?"

Lamont was clueless as usual.

The bell tinkled and the old woman who had been sitting on the park bench scuffled in. She nodded at the others and slipped into one of the plastic booths. Her canvas grocery bag was stenciled with a brightly colored rendition of the Garden of Eden, complete with apple and serpent. Filled to the top with loaves of fresh baked bread and bottles of red wine, she could barely lift it. Mickey rushed to help her.

"Thank you, young man." Her voice sounded like flat-footed detectives walking on crushed light bulbs.

"No problem, ma'am."

"You don't treat ME like that, Officer." Felicia pouted. "You don't call ME ma'am."

"That's because I don't have to threaten this nice lady to make her behave." He turned to the newcomer. "I'm your local cop. They call me Mickey the Mountain -- but I answer to Officer. Have we met?"

"I'm Sally Rubenstein. I used to live here when you weren't nothing but a squirt. I was called away about twenty years ago.

I've come looking for my husband. We have unfinished business."

"Wait a minute." Felicia sat upright.

"You are in luck, Mrs. Rubenstein. We got old Jake back in the kitchen," Lamont burst out.

"Well, I declare. What's that rascal doing back there? I've been looking for him all day." Her long white hair was twisted into a bun at the back of her head, her eyes were faded copper. Mickey rubbed his chin, trying to place her.

"He'll be surprised to see you, I'm sure." Laverne served Sally a cup of coffee and a strawberry filled powdered donut. "He used to talk about you a lot, but since his surgery he's been more closed mouth."

"He knew I'd come back."

"Officer, I need to talk to you," Felicia said.

"Twenty years is a long time, if you don't mind my saying so, ma'am." Mickey had been a cop almost that long.

"Sometimes you have to be patient -- let life work out the complications." Sally's eyes were distant. "In our case, it's been a long wait."

"Let me go talk to Jake. I'm sure he's dying to see you." Laverne's white sneakers squeaked on the linoleum as she turned toward the chrome door.

Mickey grabbed her by the elbow. "Let me."

"Officer!" Felicia stamped her foot. "Will you listen to me?"

"Sssh!" Mickey pointed at Felicia.

"Tell Jake that it's Sally. Tell him I've come back at last."

"I will, ma'am." He hit the door with the heel of his hand. Jake was hiding behind it with a huge aluminum bowl held over his head, ready to bash it down on the top of an ordinary person's head. It was chest high on Mickey the Mountain and he took it away from Jake.

"There's someone out there, Jake. Someone who's come a long way to see you."

"Lilith?"

"It's your Sally. She's come home."

"Sally?"

"She's been looking for you."

"It can't be." Jake backed into the corner.

"Well, there's a nice lady out there who claims to be Sally Rubenstein. Now why would anyone say that if it wasn't true?"

Jake rubbed his hands over his scalp. "I don't know." A joyous smile stretched across his face.

"Here, let me help you." Mickey held out his arm and Jake took it, struggling to his feet.

"Do I look okay?" He straightened his moth-eaten sweater and tucked his shirt into his corduroy trousers.

"Hold on." Mickey took a napkin and held it under a faucet. "Let's spruce you up a bit more," he said as he wiped the sleep out of the old man's eyes. "No more dreaming, Jake. This is the real thing."

"Is she still beautiful?"

"She's gorgeous."

"I used to brush her hair until it crackled like frying strawberries."

"You ready, now?"

The old man grabbed Mickey's arm. "I've changed so much. What if she doesn't' recognize me?"

"Let's cross that bridge when we have to." Mickey pulled open the door.

Sally Rubenstein turned sideways in the booth, her hunched shoulders straightening when she saw them. Pulling the pins out of her bun, she shook her head so that her hair tumbled down to her waist. "Jake!"

Jake whispered to Mickey, "I don't have my cane."

"You don't need it anymore, Jake." Sally stretched out her arms. The gnome who'd shuffled into the donut shop ten minutes before grew younger. The wrinkles tightened, the rheumy eyes brightened. Taffy colored hair floated around her face like a halo.

"Why wouldn't anyone listen?" Felicia Fry cried.

Lamont ducked behind the register, his long finger trembling over the alarm button.

Jake Rubenstein stared at the apparition that rose up before him. "Lilith!"

"No, my darling. It's me."

"Is it time?"

"Come to me, Jake."

He took two steps before clutching his chest and falling to the floor.

Sally's beauty was infinite, ethereal -- even as she faded. Mickey reached for her but she was already gone -- the scent of warm bread and strawberries all that was left of her presence.

"Is he dead?" Laverne sobbed.

"Almost." Mickey found a weak pulse in Jake's throat. At least he thought he did. "Call the paramedics, Lamont."

Lamont dialed.

Felicia Fry stood over Jake's body, her bony hands over her mouth.

"Do you know CPR?" Mickey had already started the chest compressions.

She shook her head and the wig shifted on her head.

"Close his nose, breath into his mouth when I tell you to."

"Let him go, Officer."

"NO!" He blew air into Jakes lungs before returning to the compressions. "If you won't help, I'll do it myself."

"He's gone." Trembling, Felicia sat down at the counter and took a sip of her cold coffee. "You can do that all you want, but he's dead."

Mickey the Mountain continued until the paramedics arrived. They looked at each other with doubtful eyes and continued to labor over Jake as Mickey lumbered to his feet, panting from the exertion.

"Sit down, Officer." Felicia patted the stool next to her, her flirtatious manner exchanged for a motherly one. "Laverne, get this man some hot coffee."

"Did you see it?" He held the mug in both hands.

"I saw it."

"What were you trying to tell me?"

"Sally Rubenstein died a long time ago."

"He'd been dying all day, hadn't he?" Mickey didn't like giving up. He took a quick drink and set the coffee down.

Felicia put her hand on his. "He had."

"Why didn't I see it?"

"You didn't want to."

"The ghost -- Sally. Or was it Lilith? That must have been the electrical pulses in his brain as he was dying."

She shrugged. "Probably."

"Then why did WE see it?"

"Drink your coffee, Officer."

INFINITY

Cross-legged on a gurney with a sheet wrapped around her head and shoulders, she was tiny.

"Can I come in?" I asked.

She shrugged. I walked into the examination room, the heavy door closing behind me with an airy wheeze.

"Can I sit down?"

She wasn't crying but tears weren't too far away. Once again, she shrugged. "Okay." Her voice had a tinkly, mournful Diana Ross quality.

I took off my jacket and laid it on a tall stool beside the high table. "We called your Dad," I said. "He'll be here soon. Your Mom too, but she was a couple hours away by the time we got in touch with her."

"Okay."

"You had a rough evening, huh?"

She was a tense little knot with scrawny arms and legs. I wanted to touch her but didn't. "You okay?"

She stared at her own dirty toes for a moment. "Yeah."

"I hear you did good." It was a question.

"I was bad."

"How were you bad?"

"I wanted a soda."

87

"I understand." I waited for her to work up the courage to continue.

"It was just across the street." She puckered up -- the frightened face of a guilty child. "I shoulda gone inside like I was supposed to. Mama told me to go inside right away."

"Well, you wanted a coke."

"Yeah."

I crossed one leg over the other and leaned forward to rest my elbow on my knee. It brought my face a bit closer to her. "Will you tell me about it?"

"You think he'll come back for me?" Her chin quivered.

"I don't know."

"Is the policeman still there?"

"He's standing right outside the door, Missy."

"You sure?"

"You want me to go look?"

She nodded. I pulled open the door. A tall, potbellied man, bulked up even more with a variety of police paraphernalia, stood a few feet away chatting with the receptionist.

"Jerry?" I called. "Will you come meet Melissa?" He turned and we exchanged a sorrowful glance. Jerry and I had worked together before. "Missy wants to be sure you are still here."

"You're gonna be alright, lil Miss," he boomed as he joined me in the examination room. "I'm going to be standing right out there with this billie club." He swung it at an imaginary attacker. "Ain't no one getting past me." His bravado even cheered me. Melissa held the sheet tighter around her body, but the corners of her mouth turned upwards for a second.

"Okay?" I pressed.

Her nod was almost imperceptible.

The big man winked and took up his post outside the door. I closed it and turned to Melissa. "Okay, kiddo. I have to explain a few things." My jacket fell to the floor as I crawled up onto the stool. "The doctor will be here soon. She will be looking at your body to see all the ways you might be hurt. She will touch you with her hands and some medical instruments. Her hands might feel funny because she'll be wearing rubber gloves. The instruments are metal so they might be cold. She is going to look in your mouth and in your ears and between your legs and in your butt. She doesn't want to hurt you. She just wants to make sure you are okay." The little girl trembled. I forced myself to look into her eyes. "Is your vagina sore?"

"It hurts."

"The doctor will try to be gentle, but she will need to look at it so we know if you need some medicine for it. Did he hurt your butt too?"

"With a BOTTLE!" Her eyes blazed. There ya go, I thought -- the fighting spirit. Her anger would help get her through the night.

"Okay," I said. "Are you hurt anywhere else you know of?"

"My neck." She pulled the sheet down enough for me to see the massive bruising on her long neck. "He kicked me there when I was on the ground and he jumped on it with his knees." She was furious. So was I.

"How old are you, Missy?"

"Eleven."

"Have you ever had a period?"

She looked confused. "You mean bleed?"

"Yes, bleed from your vagina."

"I did once."

"Did you hurt yourself?"

"No, I just had blood on my panties." She kept her eyes on her feet poking out from the sheet.

"Did you tell your mom?"

She shook her head.

"Okay, kiddo. I'm going to go talk to your doctor. Jerry is standing right outside your door."

Her head popped up, her eyes wide. "Don't go." She grabbed my arm. I sat back down. "You want to ask me something?"

She sniffed. "I was bad and that man hurt me."

"You want to tell me about it?"

She shook her head.

"You wanna sit in my lap?"

She scurried off the gurney into my arms, clinging to my clothes like a panicked monkey. I was startled because survivors don't usually want to be touched. Besides, this was a major no-no. I was disturbing evidence. I tucked the sheet around the trembling child and hugged her. She laid her head on my shoulder and cried. I rocked her, cooing as if she was an infant. I knew I shouldn't, but she was scared and I was the only one there.

"My mom let me out of the car at my auntie's house. I was supposed to go right in, but I wanted a soda. When my mom drove off, I walked down the sidewalk and stood at the curb waiting to cross the street. He grabbed me from behind. I fought and kicked and yelled. I swear I did."

"I know you did, honey."

"Do you think he was the boogie man?"

"He was a very bad man, Missy."

"He wanted to kill me." I could feel the terror in her body.

The doctor knocked and came into the room. "Hi, Melissa. My name is Dr. Lewis." She was short, chubby and cute. She

90

could be anybody's mom, but Missy buried her face in my shoulder. "Can you tell me what happened?" Silence. "I need to look at you, Melissa. I need to see if you are hurt."

"Remember what I told you?" I whispered in her ear. "Come on, kiddo." I stood up and set the child back on the wheeled cart. It moved slightly and she grabbed my shirt. "It's okay, I'm not leaving. I promise I'll stay right here." As I put her back on the gurney, grit and dried mud dropped onto the sheet and the floor. She was filthy.

"I'm going to start by looking at your eyes, Melissa." The doctor put a gloved thumb under each eye and studied the broken blood vessels in the white around Missy's irises.

Naked under the bright lights once the doctor pulled the sheet out of her hands, it was hard to look at Missy's beaten body. Dr. Lewis touched the huge knot at the little girl's hairline with the tip of her finger, checking to see if the mud caked in her hair was mixed with blood. Under her chin there was a two-inch scrape. Bruises encircled her neck. Both knees and elbows were raw -- and there was a shallow cut on her left thigh that had long since stopped bleeding. She squealed when the doctor manipulated her swollen pinkie. It was probably sprained or dislocated. In the small of her back was a clear shoeprint in bruises. Anita Lewis looked up at me. The bastard had stomped on this kid's back! Neither of us spoke.

"Okay, Melissa. Now we are going to take some samples of your hair. It might pull a little." With a tiny pair of scissors, Anita first snipped off several locks of matted, natty hair and slipped them into a labeled envelope. Then she pulled a few strands out by the roots.

"OW!" Missy recoiled and frowned.

"Can I look in your mouth?" As the doctor swabbed inside Missy's mouth, we both saw the white flaky substance at the corner of her cracked lips. Anita used a second swab to collect it. "You need to lie on your back now." Melissa followed instructions meekly, her anger dormant again. "I'm going to look at your vagina now so I need you to open your legs wide and put your feet up close to your butt, okay?" Melissa was too small for the stirrups.

She didn't have any pubic hair. There were a couple of curly hairs on her thigh though. Anita collected them with tweezers. Blonde pubic hairs on a black child! With gentle fingers, Anita Lewis examined Melissa's torn pudenda. The little girl squirmed and sobbed in agony. It was obvious some repair work would be necessary. In a child this young it would be done under general anesthesia I hoped. The doctor swabbed Melissa's vagina and anus. More evidence.

"There we are," I murmured. Melissa's fingers were tight around mine. I covered her with a clean sheet and peeled her fingers from my hand. "I'm just going to talk with Dr. Lewis, okay?"

Melissa nodded. She was fighting exhaustion, staying awake simply because she was afraid to sleep.

"I'll stay where you can see me."

"Okay."

I turned away from her.

"Oral rape. No question. Her vagina is bloody and full of semen. Her anus is torn up -- definite penetration with something, but no fluids that I saw. The lab will confirm," Anita whispered.

"Bottle," I said.

"God."

"And Anita, she had a period I think. She's eleven. Is it possible?"

"Of course, many kids that age have periods."

"No, I mean could she get pregnant?"

"Anything is possible."

"So what do we do?" I wasn't supposed to do anything.

She peeled off the rubber gloves and dropped them into a waste can. "This is a Catholic Hospital."

My jaw hurt from gritting my teeth. "You mean if she was brought in across town you could do something?"

"I can't here." She wrote something on Missy's chart.

"Her parents will be here soon. What if we get permission?"

"Still can't. Not here."

"You mean you would sit by and watch an eleven year old kid get pregnant? Look at that tiny body?" My voice was rising.

Anita put a finger to her lips to shush me. "I'm not the big bad wolf. She's probably not mature enough. Even if she did conceive, she'd probably miscarry. The morning after pill isn't all that pleasant for a kid -- some pretty heavy bleeding sometimes."

"A miscarriage wouldn't be all that pleasant either."

"You know the rules."

"She's been through hell, Anita."

"I know, honey, I know. Let me know when her family arrives, I need to talk with Jerry." Her polyester-covered thighs whispered against each other as she left the room.

I walked over to the gurney. Melissa was dozing in spite of herself. Sometimes sleep is the best defense mechanism available. I touched her hand and she grasped my finger like a baby. There was grit in her eyelashes and dried blood around her nostrils. We needed to clean her up. Her mother would be there soon but I let her sleep.

Jerry pushed open the door and gestured for me to join him in the hall. "Her father's in the private waiting room. You want me to help you?"

"Are her parents divorced?"

"I don't know, but the dad's pretty worried. He's waiting for you."

"Thanks, Jerry. Will you stay with her?"

"You got it."

I walked down the hall towards the waiting room filled with dread. I wondered what kind of life the kid lived. I wondered if they would support her, would love her as much as she needed to be loved. How could I prepare them for living with a rape victim? How could I prepare them for the possibility this kid might get pregnant? How could I tell them how angry she was going to be?

Two people clinging to each other watched me approach the waiting room. The woman was dressed in a crisp red wool suit. I recognized her as Marian Benston, a local TV reporter. Her brother's gaunt handsomeness mirrored her beauty. Missy resembled them both, I thought.

Marcal Benston looked to be in his mid-forties. He'd lost his left arm about four inches down from the elbow. The right sleeve was completely empty. I was shocked. Then I remembered his sister's tribute to him in a documentary about Viet Nam vets. I wondered how much tragedy an individual could endure. His deep brown eyes searched mine.

"Mr. Benston?"

"How is she? How's my baby?"

"Let's sit down, sir." I took what was left of his left arm and sat down with him. I was afraid he might fall. "Where's your wife?"

"She's coming as quick as she can. She left for a business trip this afternoon after dropping Missy off at Marian's house. I was supposed to pick her up after I finished work. Tell me, what's happened? Is she alive?" His eyes searched my soul for comfort and I had none to give. He was terrified for his child. I was too.

"She's alive -- but pretty beat up."

"Who would hurt a little girl?" His nose was running.

"Mr. Benston, there is more bad news. Melissa was raped, sodomized and beaten." The last word of the sentence trailed into a whisper as if I lost my breath. There was no way to soften that news. He crumpled into my arms. Great horrible sobs shook both our bodies as we clutched each other -- strangers made intimate by sorrow.

"Why didn't they take my TV? My car? Why'd they have to hurt Melissa?"

Marian Benston watched her brother's sorrow, her own face brimming. I locked eyes with her. She flinched as though my glance burned her. Turning, she marched off down the hall, a handkerchief held to her face, seeking privacy.

After a few minutes, Mr. Benston's sobs subsided and he pulled away. I wiped his nose with a Kleenex. His grief made such a gesture acceptable. I couldn't imagine taking such a liberty with him under normal circumstances.

"Would you like me to call the doctor?" I asked. "Maybe they could give you something to help you through this"

"No Ma'am. It took me years to get over what they gave me to help me through the pain in Nam".

It was clear he would endure whatever he had to. I shuddered at the thought of what was coming his way and wanted to delay it. But he needed to be able to take care of his family. There was no time to wait for him to deal with this. He had to deal with it now.

"Mr. Benston, the doctor will talk with you soon about your daughter's care. She's a very nice lady and will take good care of Missy. You'll have to talk with the police too -- and so will Melissa. They will talk with your wife and sister too. It won't be easy for anyone, but it will be really hard for Melissa."

"Can I see her now?" he asked.

"She was sleeping when I left, but we can see. You need to understand what Missy is going through, first. She's scared and she's hurt. She's afraid you and her mom will be angry with her for not going right into her aunt's house. She's afraid you will think she deserved what happened to her." He was horrified his daughter might think such a thing. "She is a very smart little girl, Mr. Benston. She fought back -- kicked and screamed. But he was just too big for her. After he had pinned her and raped her, it looks like he planned on killing her."

Benston moaned again and I felt like a jerk. It was my responsibility to explain to him how Missy might be, what she might need from him. I wondered if that justified this cruelty. I touched his shoulder. I didn't know how else to touch him.

"He stomped on her neck and brave little Melissa, went limp. She pretended to be dead and he left. She saved her own life, Mr. Benston. That kid is one in a million. She did what she needed to do to survive. Now she needs your support -- and your strength."

"Do they ever get over this?" He whispered as if he already knew the answer.

"No."

"What do I have to do?"

"I can tell you what to expect. I can tell you what I would do. I can tell you about services that are out there to help you. But after tonight, you'll have to figure it out as you go along." Honesty can be brutal.

"Tell me all of that then."

"At first, she's going to be under medication. That will dampen things a bit, but she's going to be in pain for awhile."

"Pain is so lonely," he murmured to himself.

I looked up in surprise. He seemed embarrassed and I continued with the required communications. There was so much to tell him. I wondered if it would do any good. I wondered if I ever did any good. I closed my eyes and suppressed the doubts. I needed to be confident. I needed to appear confident at least.

"I don't know how she'll be really. She will probably be afraid. She may even be a pain about it. Sometimes they develop rituals -- like checking all the doors and windows -- under the bed, in closets, etcetera. When they crawl into bed, they have to get up five minutes later and go through it all again. Sometimes, they think their rapists have super human qualities -- that they can come in through cracks around the door. One time, I talked with one woman who was convinced her rape was her fault because she left a window open. Turns out the window she left open was in her bathroom. It was so tiny no human could crawl through -- and it was on the seventh floor. Her rapist kicked in her door."

"What made her think it was her fault?"

"Fear," I said. "If it's your fault, you can control it. You can take precautions. Maybe you can prevent it from happening again by doing things differently. The idea of it being arbitrary is more than most folks can bear."

"Ah yes," he murmured.

"You'll have to be careful of what you say. You don't want her to think you think it was her fault but you don't want to challenge her belief it might have been until she can deal with it. Does that make sense?"

"Sort of"

"Missy may also punish herself. You will need to watch out for that. She may overeat or under eat. They think that will make them so unattractive no man will notice them -- and they will be safe. The reality is that security for them is gone. They may never feel safe again."

He bowed his head. "That was my sole wish when she was born -- to keep her safe. I didn't want her to know fear. I didn't want her to know how vicious the world can be. I just..." Tears rolled down his cheeks. I didn't know how to console him. I was only making it worse.

"She will be angry. She might break things. When appliances are out of order, she might go into a rage. She might be pretty hard to live with."

"She's my daughter. I'll love her no matter what!" He was indignant. Good for him.

Suddenly the room filled with fragrance as a pretty black woman blew in. Marcal Benston rose to meet her and they came together sobbing. He bent to hold his wife as best as he could. She wrapped her arms around his waist and held him close. They were as different as two people could be in appearance. She was tiny -- very dark -- plump, balanced on thin high heels. She turned her face up to him and I could see the bonds between them were strong. Good. They would need each other. Marian leaned against the wall in the hallway. I hadn't noticed her return. She was a lone figure and I made a note to talk with her. It's just she wasn't my first priority. Melissa was.

The Benstons sat down together. They needed a moment to compose themselves. I walked down the hall to chat with Anita and Jerry who were standing by the reception desk. Anita was writing something in a file.

"How's she doing?" I asked.

"Asleep. Are both parents here?"

"Yes. I've spoken with Mr. Benston, but Melissa's mom just got here. He's filling her in now, I guess. Has anyone talked with Marian Benston?" I asked.

"Not yet. I'll do that now if you will stand by the kid's door," Jerry said.

"Like I could keep away the boogie man..."

"She'll be looking for you if she wakes up. Just be there."

"You know I will." I found a smile from somewhere and he clomped off down the hall to talk with the elegant woman who stood apart from her family.

"How does it look?" Anita gestured with her eyes at the couple in the waiting room.

"Who knows? He seems like a good father. I think they'll be there for Melissa, they have already been through hell."

"Oh? How so?"

"Don't you remember? Marian Benston did that documentary and included her brother's ordeal after Viet Nam. A landmine or something tore off his arms -- and if I remember correctly, he was injured in the groin someway. Sylvia Benston was his nurse when he came back to the states. It took years for him to recover enough for them to get married. They were childless for years after they got married. Apparently, it was a miracle when they had Melissa."

"Damn."

"Yeah. Their miracle child is lying in there almost beat to death."

"It's a miracle that monster didn't kill her. It's going to take Jim Cartwright all night to put that kid back together. I don't think she's ever going to be right though," Anita sighed. "He's on his way here right now."

"Are you going to wait until Jim gets here before you talk with the Benstons?"

"No, but I won't be able to answer all their questions until he does. You want to sit in on this?"

"No, but I will. How do you think that's going?" I nodded towards the conversation Jerry was having with Marian. He shifted from foot to foot pausing to write something in his tiny notepad. She wrung her hands, her shoulders slumped forward inside her suit. At one point, Jerry looked up as if what she said surprised him. Then he wrote again on his notepad.

I peeked in at Melissa. She was tucked into a ball like those little bugs that curl up when you poke them with your finger. I couldn't leave her alone. I decided to stand my post, while

Anita went to Melissa's parents. I watched Anita walk up to them -- saw them rise together to greet her. My attention drifted to Jerry and Marian in the hallway as their conversation became more animated. I didn't believe in God, but I prayed anyway. "Please, God. Take care of this kid," I whispered.

I was still guarding Melissa's door when the surgeon arrived. Jim Cartwright was a round little man. When Anita called Jim, she called him because it was serious -- not because he was on-call. He was in a tuxedo and I wondered what kind of social event he had left to come join this nightmare.

"Where's Anita?"

"Talking with the parents." I gestured towards the waiting room.

"Thanks. When you gonna put some of that weight back on?" He frowned at me and strode off to join them. I watched as he walked into the room -- reaching out to shake Marcal's hand, until he realized the situation. Shocked, he grasped the tall man by the upper arm in a gesture of comfort. From time to time, Sylvia Benston shuddered or buried her face in her hands. Marcal reached out to her, stroking her gently with his stump. Something appeared to have been settled and the doctors turned away and walked off down the hall. I guessed they were going to make preparations for surgery.

Marcal and Sylvia headed my way. At first I thought they wanted to say something to me, but then I realized they were coming to see their daughter. They paused in front of the door and I stepped aside. His stump was draped over her shoulders. Her face was ravaged. He bit his lip. It was a tiny movement that broke my heart. Then they went in to see Melissa.

I glanced down the hall to see Jerry waving at me to join them. I felt torn, but then realized Missy was safe for the moment. I ventured down to Marian and Jerry. He introduced her and I reached out to shake the famous woman's hand. I felt like I knew her. I had seen her on Channel Four for years. The hazel eyes that met mine were filled with something ugly. I fancied I could smell her terror.

"Are you okay?" I felt compelled to ask.

"I don't think so."

"Ms. Benston is a little afraid of being alone right now. Would you mind staying with her a bit? I have to take care of some things," Jerry said and left us immediately. Good old Jerry leaving like that kind of unnerved me. I wondered what was so important.

"Why don't we go into the private waiting room?" I said.

She seemed relieved, "Yes, please."

We went into a small room equipped with a comfortable couch, a dim lamp and a telephone. She sat down heavily, as if she couldn't stand anymore. I sat too and waited. I didn't have a script for this.

"My poor brother", she said finally, "He's been through so much. I can't believe this has happened. Poor little Melissa." She choked back a sob.

I was silent, wondering where this was going. I sensed it was more than a concerned aunt.

"Are we safe in here?" She glanced at the door.

"Well, as safe as we are anywhere. Jerry is here -- and the hospital has guards. What are you afraid of?"

"That he'll come in here and kill me. And Missy."

I was quiet for a long moment. I couldn't believe what I had heard.

"Who?"

"I don't know his real name, but he calls himself Mingo."

"Mingo?"

"He's been stalking me for four years now. A fan gone crazy, I think." She wrapped her arms around herself and shuddered. "He has been following me, leaving messages on my email, on my phone mail, letters, notes under my windshield wipers."

"You think he hurt Missy?"

"He's been threatening me lately. I called the police. They even know who he is, but couldn't do anything. I even had a friend visit him to convince him to leave me alone. That just made him wilder." She twisted a damp handkerchief. "Last week he killed my cat and left him on my porch with a note, 'Love, Mingo'."

"Did you tell Officer Marx?" I was alarmed and afraid too now.

"Yes. I've been standing here watching Marcal go through hell and wondering if Mingo did this thing. I feel so guilty. What if I brought this down on Missy?"

"Do you have a body guard?" I asked, my heart thudding.

"No, you think I should have one?"

"My God, yes." I reached for the phone and tapped out a number I knew by heart. "Mike, can you get down to St. Luke's emergency room? Yes? No -- I mean, right now. Right. Okay. And Mike, bring help." When I hung up, my hands were shaking.

"What does this Mingo look like?"

"He's tall -- big, husky. His eyes are so light they look funny and his hair is almost white."

I thought of the blonde hair on Missy's thigh and felt sick.

"How did you meet him?"

"Well, I can't say I've ever really met him. He just started showing up wherever I was. I'd notice him on the street. One time, he was the valet for a charity event I was covering. He must have a police scanner, because whenever the news team shows up for accidents or things like that, he's there first. It was unnerving. Then he started leaving the messages. He wanted to meet me at first. Then he wanted a job on my crew. I tried ignoring him, but then he started coming to my home." Our combined fear filled the room with intensity just under panic.

"How's Missy?" she asked finally.

"Bad."

"Will she be Okay?"

"She'll live. That's not the same as being okay."

She glanced up at my face. I guessed she hoped I was exaggerating.

We sat for a few minutes until my old friend Michael found us. I introduced him to Marian and he went right into his private detective mode. I slipped out and closed the door. Police and Michael's guards filled the hallway. I was relieved. I went to Missy's room. It was empty. They had already taken her to surgery.

I went to the waiting room. It too was empty. Of course, the Benstons would be upstairs. My job was finished. It was time to go home. This was the hardest part for me. For the briefest of moments, I was an intimate part of this family in one of the worst incidents of their lives. When it was over, I often felt left out. It was silly. These people were strangers. I'd never know the end of their story. I picked up the jacket I left in Missy's exam room and put it on.

Jerry was talking with several other officers as I approached. I walked up to him, pretending to be confident. He glanced at me and then returned to his conversation -- only to glance back again. "You done for the night?"

"Yeah, nothing for me to do," I said, stalling. "Think I'll call it a night."

"Hold on and I'll walk you to your car."

I pretended to be offended he'd think I was scared. The truth was, I was grateful to him. It was near midnight and I'd parked several blocks away. "Thanks, Jerry," I said after he flashed his light inside my car, waited until I got in and locked all the doors behind me.

"Say Hi to Marv for me."

"Will do." I put the car in gear. Driving down the street, I noticed a thick figure loping towards the emergency room. I twisted my head and tried to see if he had blonde hair. It was too dark to tell for sure. As I drove out of town and headed towards the suburbs, I thought maybe the car behind me was following me, but I lost him after a series of turns.

Pulling into my drive, I was irritated with my husband. He forgot to turn the lights on for me again. Damn him, he was more worried about saving electricity than security. He just didn't "get" it. I opened the car door tentatively. Looking around, I gripped my pepper spray and dashed up to the door. The key slipped home with practiced efficiency and I was inside, flipping on lights to every room.

Marv was in the family room, watching TV in the dark.

"How are you doing, darlin?" He drawled.

"Okay, but you left the lights off again." I fought to keep the irritation out of my voice.

He stood up and put his arms around me. "Was it that bad?"

"Yes." I pushed away and went back down the hallway to the front door. I rattled the doorknob while Marv checked the windows in the front part of the house. I went down to the basement to check the sliding glass doors. I put a metal rod in the track -- I no longer trusted a wooden broomstick. We opened every closet door and rummaged everywhere someone could be hiding.

With the basement and first floor secured, we climbed the stairs and repeated the ritual on the second floor.

"Better?" Marv asked.

"Yeah, thanks, sweety." I kept the bathroom door open as I brushed my teeth and tied up my hair. I also kept it open so I could see Marv as I showered. I even kept it open when I used the toilet.

He was stretched out in bed reading a book when I came in to the bedroom. I was cold -- even in my floor length, long sleeved flannel nightgown. I crawled into bed and snuggled under his arm. He put his book aside and kissed the top of my head. I sobbed for several minutes. "Can I turn the lights out?" he asked after I had been silent for half an hour.

"No, NO -- not yet!" I almost shouted.

"It's okay. I'm here. We'll leave the lights on."

"I'm sorry, Marv, I wish things were different. This can't be much of a life for you."

"You think working at the Rape Center is helping?"

"Nothing helps."

"I know." He rubbed his hand up and down my arm.

"Will you check the basement doors, Marv?"

"Sure, baby."

ONE CHITTENDON DRIVE

I am the only constant. The students come and go but I remain -- slipping from one row house to the next by way of connected attics and holes in the basement rock walls. The six apartments, the courtyard behind them and the dumpsters in the alley -- are all mine. Columbus is not Africa, the sunny rooftop above Chittendon is not the desert -- but I survive.

• • • • •

"What is wrong with that dog?" Millie French stood in the kitchen with a box of dishes in her arms. Coco scratched at the basement door, growling.

"It's new to him too." Boris set Fluffy's large aquarium in the hallway at the foot of the stairs. The iguana blinked and tested the air with his tongue.

"No way I'm going down there. I'll wash at the Laundromat on High Street." She set the dishes on the kitchen counter.

"Suit yourself."

The iguana sneezed and bobbed his head as he caught sight of himself in a mirror leaning against the wall. "Look at Fluffy. This place gives him the willies, too," she said.

"Don't read anything into it." Boris turned the mirror to face the wall. "He does that when he moves into haunted apartment complexes."

She shook her head. "It's going to take me awhile to get used to living with a solipsistic vegetarian and a narcissistic reptile."

"Should be easy. We eat the same things."

"Fredericka knew the woman who lived in Number Three last year. She swears there's something supernatural about the whole place." Millie emptied a box of cleaning supplies.

"Is that the crone who reads tarot cards to the drunks?"

She nodded. The bars on High Street were less than a block away. All kinds of characters lined up waiting to hear their futures.

"Aha. Well, there you have it." He ducked the sponge she threw at him. "Fredericka WOULD know someone like that."

"Fredericka told me that was a sideline." She set Windex and Lemon Scented Dawn under the sink. "She was a grad student doing her thesis on poltergeists in city dwellings."

"You don't think she'd make something up to enhance the validity of her thesis, do you?"

"You are such a skeptic."

"This is a great setup, Millie. Where else are we going to get something this size this close to campus this cheap?" Boris snapped a leash onto Coco's collar and dragged him out the backdoor into the courtyard. "That takes pets."

"Bring the toaster oven in next!" She watched him tie Coco's leash to the light pole beside the back steps and head toward the alley where they'd parked the U-Haul before she closed the back door.

Dampening a sponge, she used a chair to reach the top cabinets. Wiping the shelves with Lysol, she lined them with clean paper.

The hanging light fixture swayed. Small squeaks in the boards drew her eyes to the ceiling. Something heavy was moving in the room above her. The hairs lifted on the back of her neck and she spun around. Fluffy watched her, bobbing his head.

• • • • •

Half the apartments are empty in August. Only rats and pigeons to keep me company. I never expected to find that little man in the cellar of the end unit, squatting in front of a bank of gas meters. He screamed and tried to run. Afterwards, I stretched out on the back eave where no one could see me and soaked in the warm summer rain. Now that September is waning and the fall semester has begun, new opportunities abound. I must be vigilant.

• • • • •

Millie sat at the dining room table -- a text opened to John Locke's 'An Essay Concerning Human Understanding' in front of her. Boris was in class. Fluffy snoozed in his enormous glass case. Coco snuggled against her ankles. The wind blew leaves down the street. Coco's ears perked and he ran into the living room, barking.

"Will you give it a rest?" Millie slapped her thigh but the little dog trotted back and forth in front of the window yapping. "What's wrong, boy? Scared of leaves now?"

Coco put his paws on the ledge, turning to look over his shoulder, his tongue dangling. "This better be good." She peered through the curtains. An old man hurried down the street with a sobbing child in tow. Millie opened the door and stepped onto the porch, watching as they passed. Coco dashed out to the narrow strip of grass beside the sidewalk and lifted his leg. The kid had a fresh buzz cut and was wearing coveralls.

"Who's he kidding? That's a little girl," she told Coco.

The man picked up the child and carried her into Apartment Five. A moment later, muffled screams came from behind the closed door.

Millie ran down the steps. The screaming stopped. She stood on the sidewalk, wringing her hands. "What do you think, Coco? Maybe he's her grandfather, but then again maybe he's not. What if he has a gun? Or knife?" She put her hand on the phone in her pocket.

The phone rang and Millie jumped. Flipping open her cell, she answered, "Speak to me."

"Why can't you say 'hello' like other people?" Fredericka asked.

"I'm not other people. What's going on? Is there a problem?"

"No, I called to see how you liked Creepy-Crawley Chittendon."

"I think I saw a pedophile going into Number Five with a kid."

"What exactly did you see?"

"An old man leading a little girl dressed to look like a boy. At least, I think so."

"Call 911. It's better to piss off a neighbor you don't know than to take a chance on another kid being kidnapped."

"Another kid?"

"A four year old girl disappeared off the front porch of Number Five back in the 70s. My aunt knew her mother. The poor woman nearly lost her mind thinking about what might have happened to her little one."

Millie shivered. "I think I will call, Fredericka. Hang up so I can."

• • • • •

I came to Chittendon with a zoology major who dumped her lover -- a hostile herpetologist from Cleveland. At first she was attentive to my needs. Then she found someone new -- a bushy-haired boy in a tie-dyed t-shirt and patched jeans. They took a bus to Chicago and left me here alone for months. I was younger then and much too dependent. At first I moped around the apartment. Then I found my way to the roof, scattering the pigeons that roosted there. She returned without the bushy-haired guy, but I never went back to her. She accepted that I was gone without comment. I watched her until she moved away at the end of her junior year. By then, I didn't need anyone.

• • • • •

Millie posed on the sofa. Boris concentrated on mixing his colors. "So they didn't find anyone in Number Five?"

"No one. The new tenants aren't due until mid-November. The place was spic and span. The lock broke when the last fellow moved out and the super hasn't gotten around to fixing it yet. No sign that anyone had been camping out though."

Boris touched his brush to the canvas. "You did the right thing --even if it turned out to be nothing."

"I keep thinking about that kid. I should have gone down there right then and knocked on the door."

"No one reported a little girl missing?" He loaded his brush with titanium white and a touch of cadmium yellow. The scent of oil filled the apartment and Fluffy sneezed.

"If they have, the police didn't tell me. People living in this apartment reported odd things in the past. The officer told me about a young woman who called them two or three times a week, claiming that ghosts dancing in the dining room wearing house shoes kept her awake. He told her that the way to catch ghosts was to sprinkle flour on the floor and in the morning you could see their footprints. She was busy scattering a sack of Pillsbury when they left."

Boris twirled the brush, re-creating Millie's long pale curls. "Cruel bastards."

"They said she was crazy as a loon." She shivered and sat up.

He focused on his work, adding darker tones. "She probably was, sweetheart."

She slipped on a thick pullover sweater. "I think I am too." She padded into the kitchen for a cup of tea.

"What makes you think that?" He put the handle of one paintbrush in his mouth while he worked the paint with a flat-bladed knife.

"Because I hear it sometimes too. Dozens of feet shuffling along on the hardwood floor. It goes on for a long time. Coco cringes in the hallway, whimpering. Fluffy's down here in the very next room but he never makes a sound. I fancy that he's holding his breath while the ghosts dance." She brought Boris a cup and stood behind him, examining the portrait.

"How often do you hear the noises?"

"It looks nice." She laid her chin on his shoulder as they stared at the painting together. "Not often. Every other week or so."

"Why didn't you wake me?" He dabbed at the canvas with the edge of his brush and then stepped back, squinting.

"I tried a couple of times, but you were out cold."

He turned and kissed the tip of her nose. "Give me a good pinch next time and I'll come down here and check it out. If there was anything wrong, Fluffy would be making noise, so I wouldn't worry about it."

"I'm trying not to."

• • • • •

I have my eye on that iguana. It froze when it first saw me as if it realized there was nowhere to go and I could get it anytime I wanted. The dog stays out of my way. It's too small to interest me anyway. In years past, I hung out around the dumpster in the alley outside of Unit Six looking for dog-sized rats. No passer-by ever saw me, although I once caught a mugger waiting to jump out at a pretty girl who was taking a short cut through the courtyard. That was around midnight. I was gone by morning.

Hunting is never personal. It has to do with who I find when the mood is upon me. The old man who ducked into Number Five looking for a toilet for the kid found me asleep in the bathtub. He grabbed the little girl and they ran out the backdoor before I roused myself. He must have called the police because the sirens started right after that. I was in the basement of Apartment Four when the police arrived.

• • • • •

Tears welled up in Millie's eyes.

"There, there. What's wrong?" Fredericka's smoky baritone was sympathetic.

"Coco ran away." Millie wiped her eye with her knuckle.

"I'm so sorry to hear it." The older woman put her arms around Millie.

"I came back from class yesterday and he was gone."

"Is there any way for him to get out of the apartment?"

"There must be, but we can't find it. We searched the place from attic to basement. There's no trace of him."

"Maybe he went looking for a lady friend and when he's done his business, he'll come back."

Millie blew her nose into a tissue. "I'm a mess, Ricka. I'm sorry."

"Is something else wrong?"

"It's this place. My nerves are on edge for no reason that I can explain to a practical man like Boris. He thinks I'm imagining things."

"Aw." Fredericka patted Millie on the back. "I shouldn't have put ideas in your head. Everyone has a story about Chittendon, but who knows how much is true and how much is fabricated?"

"It's not your stories. Something's very wrong here. I feel it all around me." Millie hugged herself, glancing around the room.

"What do you feel?"

"A living presence. I can't explain it, but whatever it is, it fills me with dread."

•••••

I see them through the cracks in the walls -- two women sipping from china cups, their voices a soft murmur. They are absorbed in conversation. The iguana waits for me in the dark hallway -- our destinies entwined.

•••••

"I'm sure something was in my closet the other night."

"A burglar?"

"Perhaps." Millie blew her nose. "I lay under the covers, expecting him to jump out at me if I closed my eyes. It was a war of nerves. Then he wasn't there anymore."

"Where did he go?"

"I don't know."

"Where was Boris?"

"He was down here, painting. He never heard a thing."

"Are you sure you were awake?"

"Of course, I was awake." Millie put her hands on her hips. "You think I was dreaming?"

"It's sometimes hard to tell."

"I was awake."

"Don't get upset, dear. I was only asking."

"I'm not being rational, am I?"

Fredericka held up her cup. "How about some more of that tea?"

113

The hallway and dining room was dark after the bright lights of the parlor. Millie ran her hand along the wall, searching for the switch.

• • • • •

The light flashed across me. The whipping tail of the dying iguana occupied my attention despite the screams of the women in the doorway. It was a foolish risk brought on by weeks of doing without. I released the big lizard and headed for the cellar as the women ran out on the porch.

• • • • •

"You are kidding." The policeman's face was stern.

"No, we both saw it." Millie pointed toward the ambulance where an EMT worker was administering oxygen to Fredericka. "We couldn't tell what it was, but it was huge. Big enough to kill a six foot long iguana."

"Aren't you the one who called us about a pedophile in Unit Five?"

"I called you about what I saw."

"As I remember, that was a wild goose chase."

"Ask my friend."

"Isn't she the one that tells everyone Chittendon is haunted?"

"She passes on the stories, but they are all over campus. She didn't make them up."

"Do you know how many times we get called out to this complex?"

"Go look, that's all I ask you. It wasn't a ghost. It was alive. Something big and twisted. An animal."

"I got people in there, ma'am. But I gotta tell you I'm tired of hysterical women wasting my time." The cop slipped his notebook into a back pocket. "Why don't you go over there

114

and sit down with your friend while I go see what they've found."

The breeze rattled a bush near the porch and Millie jumped. Blue and red lights flashed in the street. Drunks poured out of the bars on High and lined Chittendon watching the excitement.

"They don't believe me," Millie said to Fredericka.

"I don't believe it myself. What the hell was it?"

"I don't know. It seemed to take up the whole room."

"It was like a dragon." Fredericka shuddered.

Boris ran up to the house and grabbed a policeman's arm. The cop pointed to the women sitting in the back of the ambulance.

"Boris." Millie held out her arms, crying.

"What is it, baby? A fire?"

"Ricka and I saw something awful in the dining room. It had Fluffy."

"Is Fluffy okay?" Boris held her close. She could feel his heart pounding with alarm.

"I don't think so."

"Let me go see what's happening."

"NO! Don't go in there. Let's leave now and never go back." She clung to his hand.

"I need to go find out what's going on, Millie. You are fine. Let me go see about Fluffy."

Millie sobbed as Boris climbed the steps two at a time and jerked open the screen door.

"There are tons of police and firemen in there, he'll be fine," Fredericka held Millie's hand. "Boris can take care of himself."

•••••

I climbed into the attic through the trap door in the front bedroom upstairs, thinking about the delicious morsel lying in the dining room of Apartment One. It has been seven long weeks since the meter reader in Number Six. I was frustrated and angry. I found a dark corner in the rafters above Number Two, hoping they'd leave the iguana -- knowing they wouldn't. Maybe they'd send someone after me. One policeman -- just one.

• • • • •

The screen door swung open and Boris came out, holding something in his arms.

"Boris? Boris!" Millie tore away from Fredericka and ran toward him.

A loud yap. "Look what I found." Boris handed the little bundle over to Millie.

"Oh Coco, you sweet thing." The dog quivered with excitement, licking her face and snuggling into her arms.

"He was hiding in the front closet inside of a boot."

"Has he been there all this time?"

"Probably. It's a mess in there."

"Poor little guy. He must have seen it before we did."

"The police haven't found a thing, Millie."

She refused to look at him, focusing instead on the dog in her arms. "Not even Fluffy?"

"Fluffy was old for an iguana. It was his time to die. They get all kinds of diseases."

"How did he knock over his cage if he was so sick?"

"He was outgrowing it. Maybe he tried to crawl out. There are all kinds of explanations that don't involve a monster no one can find."

"I'm not going back in there, Boris." Millie hugged Coco.

"How are we going to find another place mid-term? The landlord will take our security deposit and the other seven months rent."

"We can sublet."

"Who will move into an apartment you are leaving because you saw a monster?"

"You guys can stay with me." Fredericka offered.

Boris frowned. "I live at Number One, Chittendon Drive, Millie. Where do you live?"

"I can't go back in there."

"What if I go through the whole place while the police are here?"

Fredericka lit a cigarette and blew smoke out her nose. "That would take hours. Look at her. She's worn out. Let me take her to my house. You can come pick her up when you've made sure that place is safe."

"Is that okay with you, Millie?" Boris rubbed the tears from her cheeks with his thumbs.

"You won't do it alone?"

"The good officers are here with me."

"Okay."

"I'll be over later." He kissed her cheek. "Don't worry about a thing."

Fredericka leaned forward. "That thing was huge. Don't go after it without a gun." She put her arm around Millie and led her away, leaving Boris standing in the street with his arms crossed over his chest.

"Yeah, sure." Boris waited until the police left before going into the apartment.

•••••

The police dispersed the crowd and the flashing lights went away. I waited a half hour after the noise died down before dropping to the attic floor. I knew Chittendon as well as my mother knew Africa. I'd been here thirty years. The coed who brought me to Columbus was more of a faddist than a zoologist. The Ball Python her lover gave her -- a small and docile species -- was actually a Rock Python -- aggressive and much larger in adulthood. Instead of the expected forty-eight inches at maturity, I grew to thirty feet alone in the hidden recesses of the Chittendon Townhouses -- feeding on rats at first, then cats and dogs -- then whatever came my way.

I emerged from the trapdoor in the closet and made my way to the top of the steps. He was down there and he was alone. I wound my way down the uncarpeted stairs of Number One, Chittendon. The basement door was open and the lights were on. Hunger drove me on as I slithered across the dining room and started down into the cellar.

SWEET MISS MARGUERITE

"Holling?"

I peered through the blinds at a half-naked woman doing aerobics in the apartment across the alley, cradling the phone under my chin. "Speaking."

"Holling, this is Samantha Rogers? I live in the same building with your mother?"

"Yes, Samantha. I know who you are." Some things in life are inexplicable. My mother's long friendship with the raging queen next door was one of them.

"It's about Miss Marguerite?"

I pressed my nose against the windowpane as my neighbor Eileen marched in place, her bare breasts bouncing up and down. "What about her?"

"It's Tuesday. On Tuesdays, I do her hair?"

I squinted, wondering if the fuzz under Eileen's lime green panties matched her strawberry blonde ponytail. "Okay."

"So I had to run down to Sally's Beauty Supply first thing this morning to get Miss Marguerite's hair coloring? She requires Pink Haze mixed with Silver Fox but all Sally's had on the shelves was Lavender Lace and that wouldn't go with Miss Marguerite's delicate skin tones at all. So I drove on down to Percy's in Oakland? To get the Pink Haze?"

"Okay."

Eileen switched from aerobics to stretching. I bit my lip, hoping she'd do the saddle stretch facing the window.

"So when I get back, I stop at my place to get my plastic cape and hair clips? I'm rushing because you know how upset Miss Marguerite gets when she's kept waiting?"

"Okay."

Eileen finished her last maneuver and slipped on her robe, omitting the saddle stretch completely.

Disappointed, I closed the blinds and switched on the TV. Denise Austin was squeezing a large pink ball between her thighs. I sat down on the couch, fascinated.

"So I knock on her door, expecting her to be bitchy about my being late?"

Samantha's habit of speaking in rhetorical questions drove me crazy. "Look, Sam. Just tell me. What's going on?"

"I'm afraid she's dead, Holling."

"Who's dead?"

"Your mother? Miss Marguerite?"

A loud buzzing in my ears drowned out Denise Austin. Marguerite was like an antique glass Christmas ornament -- pretty, multi-dimensional and well worn. I'd never let myself consider a world without her before. My eyes burned.

"Holling?"

I startled. "I'm on my way."

"Thank you, Holling."

As I drove over to Marguerite's apartment, I realized I hadn't asked the old fag what had happened to her. A heart attack? An accident? Perhaps the manner of her death wasn't important yet -- only the fact of it. The light turned green. A horn blasted. I wiped my eyes on the back of my hand and turned the corner. Washington Gardens was only a few blocks away.

"Where is she, Sam?" He towered over me in his size twelve Candies and pink bouffant wig as he let me into her apartment. He dabbed at his nose with his hanky, his large brown eyes bloodshot from crying. "In her bedroom? All tucked in like nothing's wrong?" He clasped his hands over his rubber bosom and cocked his head sideways, his delicately arched eyebrows rising over his nose in sympathy. It was nice of him, but I couldn't stand to meet his eyes just then.

I tiptoed into her bedroom like you do when you go into those fancy funeral parlors. Marguerite lay under a white coverlet with her head and arms exposed.

"Doesn't she look beautiful?" Samantha came in behind me, his perfume mingling with hers. "She wore her best satin gown. The one with the long sleeves to hide her upper arms. She was very sensitive about them since they got so flabby. Look at the lace around her wrists. Isn't that lovely?"

"She's got her makeup on, Sam."

"Don't you just love that shade of lipstick? She bought that from Elise, the Mary Kay lady, last week. The eyeliner is Mary Kay too. And doesn't that blush look wonderful on her?" Samantha sat in the brocade chair beside Marguerite's bed and touched her blushed cheek with the back of his knuckles. The two of them had been buddies for years -- two old biddies sharing their cosmetics and discussing the latest fashion pictorial in Glamour Magazine -- only one of them was six foot five and shaved his chin as well as his pits.

Her face was lovely in repose, like those old-fashioned pictures of unsmiling people in high collars. "She's wearing her eyelashes, Sam. She told me a hundred times. Make sure no one ever sees her without those false eyelashes."

"She needed a touch-up." He blew his nose. "We'll have to do something about that before the wake. She'd hate to lie in her coffin like that. With her roots showing?"

He rendered me speechless. Not because his comment was goofy, but because it was true. A sob caught in my throat. "I can't believe she's gone, Sam."

"I like to think she's here -- just out of reach." His pink acrylic nails fluttered over Marguerite's head.

I swallowed. My mother had always been out of reach. Like she floated an inch or two above the ground. Always a little different from those of us pulled downward by gravity. "Did she seem sick to you?"

"Never." Samantha was aghast at the idea. "Miss Marguerite was the life of the party even when there wasn't a party."

I realized my cheeks were wet. "How could she slip away like this? Leave without saying good-bye?"

"She couldn't help it." Samantha played with my mother's fingers, arranging them on the coverlet in an artistic display of flesh and cotton. "It was her time to go."

Samantha's mellifluous baritone broke. It was strange to see this giant illusion of femininity bent over my mother's bed, sobbing. I fidgeted, looking at the ceiling, over my shoulder at my mother's dressing table, at my feet.

The result of a high school romance, I never knew my father and my mother never married although she had a series of lovers in the early years. In the end, until Samantha Rogers moved in next-door twenty years ago, I'd been the only man in my mother's life. Even though I was never comfortable with Samantha, he and Marguerite acted like girlfriends from the very beginning. I was a teenager, eager to get out and find my own way. Samantha made it easier to leave my mother's home.

After a few moments, I cleared my throat. Samantha sat upright, his Adam's apple bobbing as he tried to compose himself. "I'm sorry, Holling. I loved your mother."

"I know." It was a weird kind of love, but who was I to judge? I was forty-two, divorced twice and lived in a bachelor pad. My sex life consisted of watching my neighbor exercise.

The only person in the world that I loved who loved me back was this vain old woman.

"We need to call someone."

"Who?" I knew he was right, but I hadn't gotten used to the idea of Marguerite being dead.

"I think her doctor might be best."

"Okay."

"You want me to do it?" Samantha stood up, tugging at his short leather skirt.

"Do you mind?" I was glad when he wobbled off on his high heels to make the call. I took his seat and reached out to touch Marguerite's hand. It was cold and I recoiled. My mother was eccentric, exotic and warm. This waxy new version of her scared me.

The day became a blur. The cops eyeing Samantha's get-up and taking notes with tiny pencils. The coroner signing the death certificate, an ugly official-looking document declaring the cause of death "Natural Causes". A black-clad fellow from Dobbs' Funeral Home putting Marguerite on a gurney and taking her out of Washington Gardens.

Marguerite made arrangements with Dobbs years ago. They had a list of instructions. Samantha was to do her hair, just as he said -- no roots for the wake. He was to do her nails too since she didn't trust anyone else to get them right. A long sleeved silvery pink gown stored in plastic, a special make-up kit and a new set of spidery eyelashes were all kept in a lock-box at Dobbs'. The only flowers allowed in the visitation room were pale pink or white -- the others were to be given to less fussy corpses.

I watched the arrangements with a mixture of amusement and sadness. Marguerite had a personal vision that only Samantha could appreciate. Dead was dead as far as I was concerned. The thought of dealing with a lot of strange people during the worst week of my life made me shiver. All I wanted to do was go home and close the blinds and watch reruns of 'I

Love Lucy' and eat Fritos and onion dip and Ben and Jerry's Chunky Monkey. If things got too bad, I'd switch to Brandy Alexanders.

"There's a note for you." Samantha held a pinkish envelope. I recognized my mother's stationary. "She left one for each of us. Carl Dobbs was supposed to give them to us after the ceremony but once I saw them, he handed them over."

I snatched it out of his hands and sat down on Marguerite's white couch. It was getting dark out. I turned on the lamp beside me.

"You want me to stay?" Samantha was eager to open his own letter.

"Suit yourself." I tore open the end of my envelope, ignoring him.

"I'll go into the kitchen then."

"Fine."

It was two sheets. Marguerite's handwriting was as delicate and feminine as she was.

"My darling Holling," she began.

I rubbed my eyes and read on.

"I enjoyed my life. The two people I love most in the world loved me enough to indulge my vanities. What more could a person want? I thank you for that.

Try to get on with your life as soon as possible. Aside from dealing with my death, there's one more thing you have to accept. A secret that I've kept for many years. Have Samantha help you find my yearbook from Saint Ambrose Academy. It's packed away in my cedar chest. Perhaps I should have told you earlier. I tried many times. It's about your father. I want you to know he didn't abandon you, Holling. I never told him about you. Life is complicated. I'm sure you know that by now. Love, Marguerite"

I sniffed and read it through a second time.

Samantha sat at the kitchen table, his long legs crossed at the ankle. He looked up from his letter. His mascara was running and his cheeks were turning bluish under his makeup. I rubbed my own five o'clock shadow. It had been a long day. "She wants you to help me find her yearbook."

"So she says." He held up his note.

"It's in her cedar chest. Do you know where it is?"

"Down in the storage room? In the basement?" He tucked his well-used hanky into his brassiere.

"Do you have the key?"

"Maybe in her jewelry box?"

I followed him into her bedroom and watched while he rummaged through my mother's things.

"This must be it." He held up a fluffy rabbit's foot key ring. "Here's the one for the storage bin downstairs. Maybe one of these others will fit the cedar chest?"

The basement storage room was dark. I found the light switch as Samantha clattered down row after row of cages, looking for Marguerite's bin. "Here it is," he called. "Over two rows?"

I traipsed after him wondering why my mother sent us on this wild goose chase. Marguerite liked to think of herself as mysterious, but there wasn't anything I didn't know about her. Even my father's name -- Roger Samson. I'd known it for years. He was a career Marine Officer. The last time Marguerite saw him, he was on his way to Viet Nam.

Samantha was inside the cage when I got there, moving boxes off the chest. Kicking off his Candies, he knelt and tried a series of keys. "There," he grunted as the third one he tried worked.

I lifted the upholstered lid. The chest was packed with scrapbooks, blankets, papers, envelopes full of photographs

125

and other keepsakes. The red leatherette yearbook was near the middle.

"It's her junior year. Nineteen fifty-nine. She had to leave school because she got pregnant with me." I thumbed through it. The pages were thick and slick. Her classmates had signed the front and back over leaves and in the margins around the glossy black and white photographs. Marguerite was a Homecoming Princess and a member of the National Honor Society. She was in Home Ec and Choir and Cheerleaders.

"She was quite a gal." Samantha sat back on his heels, watching me pick through the newspaper clippings pressed between the pages chronicling Marguerite's adventures.

"What is it she wanted me to see?" I found her photograph. Her smile was sweet, the corners of her mouth turning up without showing her teeth. Her exotic coloring -- dark hair, brows and lashes against pale blue eyes and white skin -- stood out even in the black and white photograph. As I expected, she was perfectly groomed -- not a hair out of place.

"She was so lovely then." Samantha murmured.

"I didn't know you knew her in high school." I turned to him with new interest. "What was she like?"

"Extraordinary. Brave. Strong. I was on the football squad. A linebacker, would you believe? We called her 'Sweet Miss Marguerite'. See? It's printed under her picture?"

So it was. I ran my finger over the list of her activities. I look like her even though my hair is blond and I have brown eyes. "Sweet Miss Marguerite." I sighed.

"Did you know she was my date to the prom?" The idea of this old queen taking my mother to her high school prom was bizarre. "I graduated that year and went on to college. It about killed me to leave her. She broke up with me so I'd go. There were dozens of suitors waiting in the wings. I pined for her for years. By the time our paths crossed again, things had changed for both of us. She had you and I was committed elsewhere."

It was cruel to ask him, but I needed to know. "Did you know my father?"

"Miss Marguerite never told me who he was, Holling. I'm afraid I can't help you there."

"He must be in this yearbook. Why else would she want me to see it?" I flipped through the pages, examining each male face in the junior class.

"You know his name?" Sam's face clouded. I guessed he still resented the man who left my mother alone with a baby, even after all these years.

"Roger Samson."

He paled under his rosy blush and sat back on his butt, extending his long legs in front of him.

"What's wrong?" My father must have been major competition back then. If Samantha was a linebacker, this guy must have been the epitome of male brawniness. I imagined that losing sweet Miss Marguerite to such a fellow is what turned Samantha gay. He put his hands to his face, his long square nails sliding up under his pink acrylic bangs. "Sam? What is it?"

"You are looking in the wrong place."

"So where's the right place? She told me it would be here."

Samantha lowered his hands and examined me. His gaze made me nervous as usual. He took the book from me and licked his thumb before paging through it. Finding what he wanted, he paused. "Are you sure you want to know?"

"She wanted me to know, Sam."

He handed me the book, tapping on the picture of a good-looking young man. "He was a senior when your mother was a junior."

Roger Samson had soft brown eyes. Square jawed, he had a cowlick and his greased blond hair stood up on the crown like an overgrown Dennis the Menace. He looked like every other boy in the book. Football Player, Choir, History Club, Typing. I squinted. He looked familiar.

"Were you friends with him?"

"I was his worst enemy." Something in Sam's voice made me look up.

"How do you know he is your father, Holling?"

"I've always known. His name is on my birth certificate. Marguerite says that she never told him he had a son."

He sighed. "No, she never did."

"Perhaps that's for the best." I glanced up at him, stunned.

"The question is," he murmured, "what to do about it now?"

We avoided each other's eyes neither of us accepting the sudden insight. "I think Marguerite wanted me to know in case I need a kidney or something," I said.

"Or more likely in case he gets hepatitis or AIDS." Samantha picked at a thread caught in the wire of the storage cage.

"Well, I'm in the phone book if he goes on the critical list." I closed the book and packed it back into the cedar chest, my heart pounding.

We locked up the cage and walked down the hallway to the elevator.

"Are you staying at Miss Marguerite's apartment tonight?" He pushed the call button.

"No. I have to go stop at the Stop n Go. I need Ben and Jerry's. Bad."

"Chunky Monkey?"

"Yep." We stepped into the elevator.

"You want me to close things up for the night?" He stared at his pink toenails.

128

The elevator hummed.

"Would you?"

"I'll see you at the wake, Holling."

"Okay." I got out at the lobby.

"Try to get some sleep," he said as the door slid shut.

"Right."

I sat in my car, the defroster blowing hot air on the windows, crying for Sweet Miss Marguerite and her prom date.

THE EMPTY HOUSE

The skeleton key from her mother's purse slipped into the lock. She threw her weight against the door and it screeched open. The living room smelled of old cats, old socks and old cigarettes. She opened the drapes. A beam of morning light illuminated dust particles suspended in the air.

Eleanor Billingsly had been sick for many months before she was hospitalized. She hadn't been able to clean. Cobwebs stretched across the corners of the room and moldy coffee cups sat on the end table near her chair. Stained and covered with months of debris from daily living, the carpet stunk of cat urine.

"Oh, Mama." Beth Lyons' words echoed in the empty house. Picking through the clutter left behind when someone dies, she carried three cardboard boxes of neatly filed papers out to her shiny red Volvo. She would need them to settle estate issues -- like paying her mother's taxes and bills. Eleanor hadn't owned much -- just a twelve-year-old Chevette and the house. Both had seen better days.

In the kitchen, unwashed dishes filled the sink. Beth loaded everything into the ancient dishwasher and wiped down the counters with a damp cloth. Doctor Pepper, dried-out slices of American cheese and a jar of dill pickles were the only inhabitants of the refrigerator. "No wonder you're dead, Mama." Beth, who lived on tofu and steamed vegetables, shuddered and closed the door.

In the den closet, she found empty oxygen canisters and ten cartons of Camels stacked on the floor. She thought of Eleanor towards the end with tubes up her nose, begging for a smoke. "STUPID!" she said as she threw the cigarettes into a plastic bag. "How could you do this to yourself?"

Her thin cotton blouse stuck to her damp skin. The air conditioner in the den had two speeds -- frigid and off. She struggled to open the windows but they were all stuck. The walls were nicotine yellow from the half million cigarettes her mother had smoked since the room was painted thirty years ago. She pushed open the sliding glass door and stepped out into the screened porch, setting the plastic bag full of litter on the picnic table.

A big black cat with white face and paws leapt onto the bench and hissed at her.

"Poopsey!" Beth jumped. "You scared the hell out of me."

Tail fluffed and straight in the air, Poopsey opened his mouth wide showing long sharp teeth.

"Who's been feeding you these last couple of weeks? The Lindseys?"

"Yeow!" Poopsey reared up on his hind legs and slapped at her two or three times with claws extended.

"Get real," she sighed. Beth couldn't figure out why Eleanor loved this ill-tempered beast. He knocked over every knick-knack in the house with a disdainful swipe of his paw and left little turds in the shower whenever he got mad.

She rummaged through the pantry until she found a small box of Meow Mix. She filled his dish and set out a small saucer of water. The cat hurried over to the water and lapped loudly. He sniffed the food and walked away without touching it, his tail in the air.

"That's all that's here, you stupid cat."

"GRRR," Poopsey answered before walking stiff-legged down the hallway.

"We don't HAVE any little cans of 'Liver N Bacon'!" Beth called after him.

Looking over his shoulder with a malicious glint in his yellow eyes, Poopsey lifted his leg and sprayed the bathroom doorjamb.

Beth slammed the box of Meow Mix down onto the counter. The cat flipped his tail at her and went into Eleanor's bedroom.

• • • • •

It took two days to empty the house. Beth packed Eleanor's books and took them down to the Half Price bookstore. Thirteen cartons netted the estate $152.17.

Beth didn't know anyone who could wear Eleanor's size twenty-four dresses so she donated them to Good Will along with a box of shoes and some unworn, uncharacteristically frilly underwear. She threw her mother's stretched-out cotton panties and huge old-lady bras away. Who would want to wear a dead woman's underwear anyway?

Aunt Verna agreed to take the mismatched china, but the upholstered furniture was a mess. Poopsey had rubbed against Eleanor's expensive brocade drapes, sharpened his claws on the couch and slept in the recliner. Beth took everything to the dump outside town.

The maple piano, end tables, coffee tables, bed, nightstands and dresser went to the next-door neighbors who paid the estate a grand total of $250.

The stuff she wanted to keep like the contents of the linen cabinets, her mother's collection of antique salt and pepper shakers, jewelry and the family photos, she packed into the Volvo. The rest went out on the edge of the driveway for the garbage men.

Poopsey crouched on the piano for most of the two days, watching her work. Twice he laid in wait as she came down the hall with her arms full of boxes and sprang up to dig his claws into her buttocks. Once he stalked her from room to room and when she bent over to retrieve her parents' marriage license from the cedar chest, he dashed out from under the bed and bit her ankle. Beth screamed and kicked at him. "YOU'RE A MENACE!" Poopsey dodged the kick and trotted off to hide in the den.

By the end of the second day, Beth had found a home for all of Eleanor's possessions save one. Poopsey. Her second-cousin-once-removed agreed to take him, but when one of the kids tried to pick him up, Poopsey hissed and slapped her face three times. Thank heavens he kept his claws retracted. The little girl was terrified and ran sobbing to her father who subsequently backed out of the deal. Beth thought about sending the vile feline to the pound, but Aunt Verna cried and begged her not to send the poor pussy to his death. Aunt Verna was allergic to cats of course and couldn't take him herself.

At dusk, Beth sat down on the floor of the screened-in back porch with a dishtowel thrown over one shoulder, a bottle of distilled water in one hand and a watercress sandwich in the other. Poopsey sat just inside the door watching her with malevolent eyes.

"It won't work out between us, buddy. The only reason we ever put up with each other anyway was Mama. And she's dead. So it's over."

"GRRR!" He put his ears back.

"I'm glad you agree. I'll be out of your hair here in a few minutes. Only thing is I'm selling this house so you have to leave too."

The cat growled again.

"Don't even think about it. I'm a vegetarian. You are a carnivore. I like things to be clean and neat. You are a slob. I don't want to come home to find hair balls on my carpet."

"ARRR!" Poopsey seemed to dislike her as much as she disliked him. Fine!

"There are tons of field mice and black snakes and bird nests around here. The pond is over the hill if you want a drink. I'm sure the Lindseys will feed you in a pinch. Stay away from the traffic on State Line Road and you'll be fine."

The cat twitched his tail from side to side. Beth stood up and opened the screen door. "It's time for both of us to get out of here."

The cat stretched but made no move to go outside.

"Come on, you good-for-nothing horse's petoot." Beth held the screen open and gestured with her head towards the backyard.

Poopsey gazed out the door as if fascinated. He took one step forward. A bat flew in, fluttering around the porch making weird screeching sounds. The cat rose up on his hind legs pawing at what appeared to be a winged mouse several feet above his head.

"Yuk!" Beth swung the dishtowel at the bat to encourage it to move back towards the door. As it flew into the yard, Poopsey raced after it snapping his jaws. Beth slammed the screen behind him and hooked it.

"There!" She dusted her hands off against each other and sighed in relief.

Gathering up the last few boxes of odds and ends, she locked the front door and trudged out to the car. Even though it was loaded to the roof with Eleanor's possessions, it still had that new car smell. She put it in gear and started down the long driveway, the gravel crunching under her tires. Halfway down the lane, she stood on her brakes. The middle leaf of Eleanor's kitchen table slid forward to hit her in the back of the head. She cursed and put the car in "Park".

Poopsey sat in the middle of the drive licking his hindquarters.

"What do you think you are doing here? Didn't I tell you to get lost?" Beth got out of the car rubbing her head. Poopsey looked up at her and bared his teeth in a silent snarl.

134

"It's over. No little cans of 'Liver N Bacon', no nutty old woman to put up with your moods and your messes, no expensive furniture to destroy. She split, buddy. There's nothing left -- nothing but an empty house." She threw a piece of gravel his way. It hit the ground in front of him. He galloped off into the weeds that had taken over Eleanor's flowerbed in the side yard.

• • • • •

Three days later, Beth was back in her office in Cleveland. Her desk was stacked high with work that went undone the three weeks she'd watched her mother die. She was in a foul mood when the phone rang around eleven o'clock in the morning.

"This is Beth."

"Miss Lyons, this is Barbara McNally from Owens Realty? You asked me to get someone to clean your mother's house?"

"Yes, Mrs. McNally. What can I do for you?"

"We have a problem here." The woman paused.

The moments ticked by in silence. Beth said, "And, the problem is?"

"I sent one of our best people out to clean. Ruta Mae Belle? She's been working for us for years. We never had a problem before now."

"Look, Mrs. McNally. I know that house is a mess. I don't blame Mrs. Belle if she wants a little more money to clean." Beth wouldn't want to touch the place herself what with the cat odors, the acrid smell of stale smoke and the mildew. She was embarrassed Eleanor chose to live that way. Her own tiny apartment was pristine -- smelling of vanilla candles and room fresheners.

"Oh no, I didn't mean to mislead you, it's not that. We often use Mrs. Belle to clean estate homes before sale." Mrs. McNally paused again.

"So what's wrong?" Beth tapped the eraser of her pencil against her desk blotter.

"She knew someone died and that old house is so big and as you say, it doesn't smell so good. She was just starting to mop the kitchen floor when she heard this unearthly sound echoing throughout the house. She dropped her mop and left her bucket and all of her cleaning materials where they lay and ran out of that house like the hounds of hell were on her heels. She said she could hear it all the way at the end of the drive."

"What did she think it was?" Beth sat up in alarm. Was someone hurt? Was there a burglar?

"Well, uh -- ma'am, she thought it was a ghost."

"A GHOST?"

"She says she won't go back."

"A GHOST?" Beth was stunned. For a moment, she wondered if maybe Eleanor -- no, that was ridiculous. "Surely you don't believe in ghosts, Mrs. McNally?"

"Of course not. But Ruta Mae does and she's got all the other ladies scared. No one wants the job now."

"I see."

"What do you want me to do?" Barbara McNally's voice quivered.

"I want you to go see what's wrong. And hire someone to clean so we can sell that damned house." Beth fought to keep the irritation out of her voice.

"I -- uh, well, okay."

Beth hung up the phone and took deep breaths. This was just what she needed -- some neurotic cleaning lady running her mouth and scaring away buyers.

• • • • •

"Miss Lyons?" The voice on the other end of the line burbled with laughter.

"Is that you, Mrs. McNally?" Beth was eating a salad and sipping green tea.

"It was a cat, Miss Lyons. A big old black and white tom crawled under the house and got stuck in the heating vent. Didn't look like he'd had much to eat lately -- and he was scared. Like to took my hand off when I found him. The Lindseys say he was your mother's cat. He must have been hiding while you were here."

"Yeah, he must have been hiding."

"What do you want me to do with him?"

She didn't have much choice. "Put him in a box and deliver him to the airport. I'll have a ticket waiting for him."

"Should I take him to the vet for a sedative?"

"I don't know," Beth admitted. She'd never even had a roommate, let alone a pet.

"It might be better for him. He's pretty agitated right now. The plane will scare him even more."

"Do what you think is best and bill me." Beth couldn't imagine poking a pill down that ugly beast's throat.

• • • • •

When Beth got to the airport, she took her place at the end of the line at the baggage claim counter. Glancing at her watch and looking around, she caught the clerk's eye. "KITTY CAT?" She mouthed.

The clerk beckoned her forward. The whole line moved aside. As she approached the counter, she heard the screaming. The clerk handed her a small pet carrier. Poopsey howled and threw himself against the sides.

"Poor cat took off in seventy degree weather and flew to Dallas where it was eighty-five degrees. Then he flew here where it's twenty-seven degrees. What do you expect?" The clerk scowled.

"I don't know anything about cats." She felt she had to explain. The clerk shrugged and turned to the next customer.

Poopsey continued his caterwauling as she walked towards the exit. The angry eyes of animal-loving travelers scalded her as she passed them. "Why did you do this to me, Mama?" She put the frightened cat in the back seat of the car and drove through the icy streets to her apartment.

Beth opened the door to her apartment and sat the carrier down on white carpet. Poopsey crouched and sniffed the air, his screams turning into low growls.

"Come on out!" She unfastened the carrier door and went into the kitchen. Looking over her shoulder, she opened a little can of 'Liver N Bacon'. Poopsey crept forward on his belly until he could see her around the corner. "I told you you wouldn't like it here." She put the food in the new bowl she bought on her way home from work and set it on the white tiled floor.

Hissing, Poopsey dashed across the hallway and hid under her living room sofa.

"Fine. Have it your way. I'm going to bed. Don't you DARE pee on my carpet." Closing the door behind her, she crawled into bed and pulled the covers over her head.

Beth awoke at two o'clock in the morning. A baby was crying somewhere in the apartment complex. A long, mournful wail. This was an adult building. There weren't supposed to be any babies. Where were its parents? Who'd leave a baby alone? Crying like that?

Rubbing her eyes, she headed for the kitchen for a bottle of distilled water. The sobbing got louder when she opened her bedroom door. It was then she realized it was Poopsey.

She wandered through the apartment following the sound of his voice. She found him in the small storage room under the stairs where she'd stacked boxes of her mother's possessions. He sat in the one holding the sheets off Eleanor's bed -- his head back, howling.

"What's wrong with you?"

The cat's voice raised chills on Beth's neck.

She sat cross-legged on the floor -- hating Poopsey. Hating that Eleanor spent her last years in a filthy house with this obnoxious beast. Hating that her mother let herself die. Hating that she hadn't been there to save her.

The cat's eyes glowed in the semi-darkness of the closet. Beth found one of Eleanor's pillowcases. Maybe she'd use it to smother the cat's shrill voice. Maybe she'd strangle him with it.

The pillowcase smelled of Eleanor's cigarettes and Eleanor's shampoo and Eleanor's skin cream. Beth held it against her face. "Oh, Mama." Her nose burned as the tears finally started. Rocking back and forth, her sobs blended with the howls of a stupid black cat.

THE RUBBER DOME

When Margaret Evers decided to re-activate her love life, she created a folder on her computer called "Sex" with subfolders named "Requirements", "Potential Partners", "Resources" and "Birth Control". Scheduling four hours a week to focus on the endeavor, she developed a detailed project plan. After all, she was a busy woman.

It was six years since she lost her husband to a car crash. In all that time, she remained celibate -- convinced she would never be able to love again, her heart burned beyond recognition along with Malcolm.

For a month after Malcolm's death, she crushed his pillow to her face -- comforting herself with his dissipating scent until the housekeeper changed the bed linens. That night, she had to accept that he was never coming back.

She was different now -- a dedicated executive. Thank goodness for her job. It kept her busy all day every day. She was content for a while -- but after her son left for college, after her last promotion, her thoughts turned to sex.

First, a vague restlessness wafted like a cool breeze through her room at night. Her lips and nipples began to tingle. Then the dreams started. Dreams of Malcolm. He came to her naked, his erection bouncing as he walked. He threw back the covers with a flourish grinning at her with a mischievous glint in his eyes. She welcomed him with open arms and open legs, gasping with pleasure as he entered her -- screaming with joy as he began his climax, convulsing with her own orgasm as he whispered words of love into her ear. She awoke with a start -- empty and alone.

One night, it occurred to her that she could have sex without love. Men did it all the time she understood. Perhaps she could find a male body she could use. Perhaps she could pretend he was Malcolm.

She labored over her requirements. The man would have to be older than her. She felt maternal around younger ones. He would have to be married. She didn't want him falling in love. She was five foot six -- that meant he had to be at least five foot ten. He didn't have to be handsome. She preferred a rough earthiness -- a man with thick fingers and a heavy beard. He had to be healthy. She didn't want to deal with impotence or anything she could catch. Personality didn't matter. There wasn't going to be much talking. He was to act as Malcolm's stand in. Nothing more.

Margaret knew there would be no problem finding candidates. It was a good deal for most middle-aged married men -- a free roll in the hay with no complications. They wouldn't even have to pay for a hotel room. Besides, she had been attractive before her heart died. She was used to queries from interested men.

Birth control was another issue. When their son was born eighteen years ago, Malcolm got a vasectomy. That decision left her vulnerable in her present circumstances. Unwilling to trust a man with this responsibility, she visited her gynecologist and brought home a diaphragm which she stored under the sink in her bathroom.

Preferring a stranger, she posted ads in the newspapers and on the Internet. Within a week, she had fifty-two applicants. She sorted through them sitting cross-legged on her king sized bed. There were three piles -- the 'absolutely no way in hell' pile was the largest. Thirteen applicants made it to the 'Not likely but possible' category, while three landed in the 'Interview!' group.

For safety sake, she rented a small hotel room set up with a long table, comfortable chairs and no bed. If a candidate passed the first meeting, she would invite him to her home.

Candidate number one was a salesman who traveled through her city once a month. His family lived in Atlanta over a thousand miles away. He was six foot tall with no distinguishing marks. He claimed to be an accomplished athlete who would service her with a variety of positions. He denied any interest save the sexual one.

Herbert Alby arrived at the appointed hour looking younger than the required age of fifty. Carrying a black leather portfolio about the size of a briefcase, he wore a pinstriped navy suit with a light blue shirt and a plain, red silk tie.

"Good Morning, Mr. Alby." Margaret leaned across the table to shake his hand.

"It's nice to meet you, Ms. Evers." His voice cracked. "I have to admit that I've never approached a sexual liaison in quite this way and I'm a little nervous. The first meeting usually takes place in a bar."

"No need to be nervous, Mr. Alby. Please have a seat." He sat down and crossed his long legs.

"I have a list of questions to ask you. There is no right or wrong answer, just your answer, okay?" Her smile was warm. She could see him relaxing and growing more confident.

"Okay, Ma'am. Ask away."

"Mr. Alby, do you smoke?"

"Well now, I've never looked to see." His broad grin faded. "Sorry, Ma'am. I was trying to be funny."

"No need to be funny, Mr. Alby," she sighed.

"Yes Ma'am. No Ma'am, I don't smoke."

"Do you have a sexually transmitted disease?"

"Oh no, Ma'am. I'm as healthy as a horse." She made a large check mark on the paper in front of her.

"Would you be willing to be examined by a doctor of my choosing?" She peered at him over gold-framed half glasses.

"Uh, well. I guess. Sure. Okay." He squirmed in his seat.

"How many sex partners are you currently maintaining?"

"One. Two. But not very often. Well, maybe only one. My wife." He ducked his chin and stared at his polished black loafers. She made a notation in the margin of her paper, 'Doesn't know how many people he's sleeping with!'

"You state in your application that you are a sexual athlete. What does that mean?"

"It means I do everything my partner requires. Oral, missionary, doggie, anal. I brought you references and pictures." He unzipped his portfolio and laid it open on the table. The pages were encased in plastic and he turned them slowly as she read. The first one was written in purple ink and it said, 'To Whom It May Concern, Herbie Alby is good in bed.' It was signed 'Lorna Leroy' and underneath her name was a smiley face. The second one said, 'Herbert Alby is one great lover!!!' and it was signed in black ink by 'Marian Myers'. Margaret noticed that Lorna and Marian had the same handwriting and both had alliterative names. Marian did refrain from the smiley face though. The next page showed a full-length photograph of Mr. Alby in the nude with his hands crossed over his genitals. The next showed his back and naked buttocks. The last page was a glossy eight-by-ten close-up of a smallish penis.

"Aha." Margaret leaned back in her chair and wrote something on her paper. Herbie closed his sample case and zipped it.

"As you can see, I'm in good shape and I believe I can do the job you described."

"Thank you, Mr. Alby. I'll be in touch." She stood up. He stood up.

"I'm really very good."

"I'm sure you are. Thanks for your time, sir."

He took her hand and lifted it to his lips, kissing the palm. "You are tense, Ms. Evers."

She showed him the door. "Thank you, Mr. Alby."

The next man on the list was a retired truck driver. Allan Trembly opened the door a few inches and peeked inside. "Is this where I'm supposed to be?" His colorless eyes hid inside the folds of his lids.

"Are you Mr. Trembly?" Surprised, Margaret consulted her schedule.

"Reverend Trembly, actually." He shut the door behind him. The clerical collar cut into his thick neck and his pullover sweater rode up high on his huge belly. He carried a ragged shopping bag in his left hand with faded butterflies printed on the side.

Margaret was a professional interviewer. She took this unexpected hitch in stride. "Please have a seat, Reverend Trembly."

"Thanks, missy. It's good to get a load off."

"I have a series of questions. Are you ready?" Using her thumb, she clicked her gold pen open and closed several times.

"Ask away." He rummaged in a back pocket and withdrew a beat-up pipe. He turned it upside down on the table and hit it a few times. Crumbles of partially burnt tobacco and ashes spilled out onto the white cloth. "Oh, I'm sorry," he said when he saw her face.

"Why you are here, Reverend?"

"When I read your ad, I recognized a soul in distress. I came to offer my Christian testimony."

"Reverend Trembly, you lied on your application!"

"Just a tiny one." He held his thumb and forefinger a half inch apart. "I was afraid you wouldn't talk to me if you knew I was the mouth of the Lord." He poured fresh tobacco into the pipe bowl.

"If you plan on lighting that thing, please don't."

Flushing, he put the pipe away and rummaged in the shopping bag. "I brought you some brochures to tell you about the Lord. If you take the time to read them, you'll be comforted."

She folded her arms over her chest. "I have my own religion."

"Give yourself to Jesus, missy. It will change your life."

Margaret stood up. "This interview is over, Reverend."

"We could have a bible class right here." He pulled a small black book from the shopping bag and opened it.

"Thanks for your time, Reverend." Her bright red fingernails dug into his flabby biceps.

"OUCH!" He whimpered as she escorted him out.

She had just reached her seat when someone knocked.

"I forgot my shopping bag," he called.

She jerked open the door and pushed the bag into his arms.

"You DO have a nice ass." He made a quick grab for her buttock. She slammed the door on his fingers.

The third applicant owned a hobby shop in a small town thirty miles to the north of her. He was the only one of the three who wasn't married. His wife had died a lingering, horrific death from emphysema three years ago. However, he assured her he had familial obligations and wasn't looking for a relationship, just sex.

He did well in the interview and even though he wasn't much taller than she was and sported a big belly, he seemed safe and agreeable. She invited him to her home.

When Sam Beaumont rang her doorbell, Margaret was naked under her sheer black robe. His eyes clung to her breasts

145

as she led him to her bedroom. Heavy velveteen drapes darkened the room. The coverlet on her bed was turned down and rose petals were sprinkled over the sheets, but she drew him to the loveseat first.

"Ms. Evers -- Margaret --."

"Don't say anything," she warned.

"But Margaret, you are so --."

"How can I pretend you are Malcolm if you keep talking?" She put her arms around his neck and pressed her mouth against his. He responded by pulling the clasp out of her bun. Her hair fell over her shoulders and down her back.

She inhaled. He wore the required aftershave. Malcolm's. She accepted his tongue. It tasted so good. Felt so good. The kiss became more passionate. On cue, as if he knew it was time, he cupped her left breast and moved his lips down her neck.

Her heart thudding in her ears, she luxuriated in the feel of his hands on her breasts and imagined that her darling Malcolm had come home. The point of no return was approaching. It was time to put on the brakes.

"I'll be back in a minute. Fold your clothes and put them on the nightstand there. Shush!" She held her finger over her lips and backed naked into the bathroom.

It was poor planning. She realized that now. When she decided to delay putting in the diaphragm, she wanted a way out in case things weren't going well. This man played his part perfectly though and the interruption frustrated both of them.

Arousal made her clumsy. The pink plastic case cracked when she dropped it into the sink. She rinsed the small rubber dome under the tap. As she slipped the rim onto the tip of the insertion stick, she missed and it fell on the floor. "Damn!" She picked it up and rinsed it again.

She could hear Sam pacing out side the bathroom. She imagined Malcolm's impatience. "I'll be right there, just a

146

minute," she called as she reattached the diaphragm to the insertion stick.

Using her teeth to loosen the lid on a tube of spermicide, she coated the rim with jelly. To be doubly safe, she filled the inside of the cup too. Was that the inside? She wasn't sure. She squeezed an equal amount on the other side. Springs squeaked outside as Sam sat down on her bed.

The next step was to put her foot on the edge of the commode and slip the stick with the diaphragm attached to it up inside her. Feeling foolish, she smothered a giggle. Who came up with this idea, she wondered. Taking a deep breath, she squatted and twisted the stick. The rubber dome popped loose too soon and skidded across the bathroom floor. She laughed aloud as she got down on her hands and knees to chase it.

"Are you all right?" Sam called.

"Fine!" The dome squirted out of her hands and became airborne, sticking to the top of the shower door, way out of her reach. She jumped, her heavy breasts bobbing and her bare feet thumping on the ceramic tile.

"What's wrong?" Sam stood naked in the open doorway. A short pot-bellied middle-aged man, his erection was gone and his soft penis dangled in front of him.

"Look!" Margaret pointed at the diaphragm stuck on the shower door, her eyes dancing. She jumped again, trying to knock it loose. Sam's eyes went from the greasy rubber cap stuck on the shower door to Margaret. A slow grin creased his face.

"Let me try." He stood on his toes and stretched. He couldn't reach it either. He jumped -- his penis waggling as he landed. Margaret's laughter was contagious and he chuckled too. He tried again, the tips of his fingers hitting the diaphragm and breaking its suction on the glass. It flew across the room, bouncing off the windowsill and landing on Sam's foot.

Margaret wrapped her arms around her mid-section, gasping for breath. Sam peeled the slippery piece of rubber from his instep and tossed it in the sink.

"Now THAT'S what I call showing a fellow a good time, Margaret." He put a thick arm over her bare shoulders.

Their laughter melted into embarrassed silence.

"What do you do when you find a naked man in your bathroom?" He leaned in to kiss her, but she flinched.

He sighed.

"I'm sorry, Sam. This isn't what I expected or planned for."

"I guess the spell is broken, huh?" He squeezed her shoulder and withdrew his arm.

"Thank you for trying." Margaret lowered her eyes.

"We could try again." He touched her nipple. It remained flaccid.

"How can I pretend you are Malcolm now? I'll always picture you jumping up in the air naked." Her eyes twinkled at the memory.

"Maybe you would consider making love to Sam."

She kissed his cheek and pointed toward the bedroom. "I don't even know you."

His shoulders sagged. He went to her bed and picked up his clothes. She leaned against the doorjamb of the bathroom watching him dress, amused at the culmination of this non-affair.

He caught her eye and grinned. "I know a fun way for you to get to know me."

She shrugged. "I'm empty, Sam. I have nothing left to give. I'm just a horny old broad. Not much of a bargain."

"I'm willing to give it a shot."

He was sweet, but he wasn't Malcolm.

"It was a silly idea anyway." She helped him put on his shirt. "I don't want to ever feel the way I did when Malcolm died. I want to control things so they don't control me."

He nodded and zipped up his pants. "You know my number if you change your mind. I can let myself out." His footsteps receded down the hall.

Her eyes drifted over to the bed. It was a vast lonely plain -- the sheets smooth except for a slight wrinkle where Sam had sat.

Life was rich when Malcolm was in her bed. She'd cuddle up behind him, loving him with her flesh -- caressing him with her mouth and breasts and weeping vagina. How could she ever let that go?

The mirror caught her eye. There was a small red mark on the side of her neck. She smiled. She hadn't had a hickey since she was seventeen and they called them monkey bites. The woman in the glass was forty-eight years old. Malcolm was gone, but there was a lot of her life left to live.

She closed her eyes. Laughing with Sam felt so good -- almost better than kissing him. No. Kissing was good too.

"Oh Malcolm," she sighed, relaxing her grip on the edge of the sink. "Goodbye, my love." Grabbing a thick robe, she got to the door just as Sam was getting into his Volvo.

"SAM! SAAAAAAM!"

"What?" He stuck his head out the window.

"Want a cup of coffee?"

THE MENAGERIE

Cleveland, Ohio – 1942

Pam Kline squinted against the bright sun when she stepped outside the Terminal Tower. It was mid-morning on Public Square. Taxis, buses, trucks and cars filled the streets with blue fumes and beeping horns. She froze in the middle of the sidewalk, momentarily disoriented, as people swirled around her, many of them in uniform.

"Well, don't stand there, goober. Let's go find us a circus." Danny gave her a nudge. She scowled and pushed back. He might be dressed up in his sailor suit, but he was still her brother. The last time they came to Cleveland, it was to see a ballgame. That was only a few months ago. She'd never even heard of Pearl Harbor then.

They crossed the square and headed east on Superior. She struggled to keep up with him, a dog-eared copy of the Ringling Brothers and Barnum & Bailey magazine for 1942 under her arm. A painting of two elephants dancing was on the front cover. She wondered if one of them was Ringling Rosie. She'd never seen a real elephant, let alone an elephant ballet.

They turned left on East Ninth Street and headed towards the lakefront, her excitement growing with every step. They had money in their pockets. Since the war started, everyone had jobs again and their father's business was good. However, they were planning on getting into the 'Greatest Show on Earth' for free -- Danny, because he was wearing his uniform,

150

Pam because she would agree to crawl around under the bleachers collecting coke bottles dropped there by last night's audience.

The circus was set up on a lot not far from the municipal stadium, squeezed in between the bluffs below Cleveland and the railroad tracks. As elephants unloaded posts and canvas from the gaily-painted train, large ships waited for wartime cargos of steel in the glittering lake below them.

"Hurry up," Danny urged her as he disappeared over the crest of the hill.

"I AM hurrying." She ran to catch up, the calves of her legs aching. It wasn't fair. He always left her behind. He probably was meeting some of the guys down there or maybe a girl.

As Pam fought to keep her balance on the gravely slope, she saw Danny leaning against a fence just outside the midway smoking a cigarette. A large poster behind him proclaimed, "One Hundred Clowns, One Thousand Animals." He waved and made faces. She stuck out her tongue and trotted up to the ticket booth.

"Ain't you a purty lil young'n?" An enormous woman in a flowered dress held a large roll of tickets. "Doors don't open til one o'clock unless you wanna collect up the empties. You payin or trollin' fer bottles?"

"Trollin'," Pam said and pocketed her pass. She glanced over her shoulder at Danny. He was talking with another guy in a brand new uniform. Army, Pam guessed. They made whooping sounds whenever one of the circus women in their tight fitting costumes wandered across the lot. She KNEW it. Danny had other plans. She kicked a piece of gravel and it went skittering across the road.

"Go on down to the Big Top. It's that red and white tent just beyond the Menagerie. You gather up the empties and put 'em in that striped box across the way there. Ya see it?" The ticket lady was nice enough, but Pam had never seen anyone quite so hairy before. One thick brow covered both eyes and

151

she had dark hair on her cheeks and a thin mustache. There was even hair on the tops of her football-sized breasts where they bulged out of the neckline of her dress.

"Yes, ma'am. I see it."

"That sailor boy related to you?"

"Yes, ma'am. That's my brother, Danny. He's leaving for San Diego tomorrow."

"I ain't sposed to let you do this, but you tell him he and his friend can go on in with you if he wants. None of the sideshows will be open yet, but you can see the animals and talk with the circus folk after you are through with them bottles."

"Is Ringling Rosie here?"

"She's here alright." Several of the woman's hairy chins jiggled as she laughed. "Everybody wants to see that sweet lil elephant. She's in the Menagerie right there waiting for her lunch."

Pam couldn't help but examine her own forearms for any telltale hair growth as she waved the two boys in. They crushed their cigarette butts beneath their boots and loped along beside her.

"Bennie Bermeister, I'd have never recognized you in that getup," Pam said to the tall, pimply-faced young man who draped his arm around her shoulders. His breath smelled like sour chocolate and she wrinkled her nose.

"How ya doing, half-a-chunk?" Bennie patted her head like she was a puppy.

She HATED when he did that. "Cut it out!" She pulled away and punched him in the side.

"You're growing up now, aren't you?" He pinched her cheek. "Don't you think you oughta trade in them overalls for a dress?"

She slapped at Bennie with both hands, dropping her magazine in the dust. "Take your hands off of me." He backed away as she advanced on him like a militant windmill.

"Aw, Pam, don't be such a stick in the mud," Danny grabbed her from behind, pinning her flailing arms to her sides and lifting her up off the ground. "Don't you know when you are being teased?"

"He ain't got no call doing me that way." She kicked and squirmed.

"No, he sure doesn't. He's sorry and he's not going to do it again, ain't that right, Bennie?" Danny frowned at Bennie who flushed and nodded. "You gonna be good if I let go of you, goober?"

"What's he doing here anyway?"

"I came to see the circus, same as you." Bennie tipped his cap over one eye and dusted off his hands like that uniform made him a big shot or something.

"Doesn't mean you have to follow us around." Pam had no use for Bennie. He had teased her since she was six years old -- taking balls away from her and holding them over her head, or kicking over her Tinker Toy creations.

"Pam, you behave yourself," Danny admonished her.

"I mean it, I don't want him around."

"Fine, I'll go look at Gargantua all by myself." Bennie turned on his heel and disappeared into the Menagerie Tent.

Danny let go of Pam and she turned on him. "I'm too old for you to keep holding me back that a way, Danny Kline!"

"You're too old to act that way. I thought we were gonna have a good time and we ain't even in the door before you are picking a fight with Bennie."

"I thought you were taking ME to the circus." A tear rolled down her cheek. "You're going to war tomorrow and you wanna spend the day with HIM?"

Danny handed her his handkerchief. "I don't wanna spend the day with him, he just showed up."

She blew her nose. Her sock had slipped down inside her scuffed saddle shoe and she bent to straighten it. "Then let's leave him here." Danny always chose his friends over her. ALWAYS. She picked up the circus magazine, rolled it up and stuck it in her back pocket.

"Okay. Let's go take care of those bottles before the sideshows open." He took her hand. She'd wanted to go see Ringling Rosie first, but she wanted to get away from Bennie Bermeister more.

A mild circusy smell -- fresh hay, even fresher manure, and overripe bananas -- drifted over them as they passed the Menagerie. A bald-headed midget handed them a flour sack as they went into the Big Top. Three other kids were clambering around under the bleachers to the left, so Pam and Danny started on the right. Cool air chilled their cheeks. It was air-conditioned. Pam held up her palms, turning slowly to feel the sweat drying on her forehead and under her chin. "I never been in an air-conditioned tent before."

"There's lotsa places you never been." Danny held out the sack and she dropped the first bottle into it.

They worked for several minutes, filling the bag with clinking glass. She thought about Danny on a ship halfway around the world. As usual, he was leaving her behind. What if he didn't come back? Maybe this was the last time they'd go to Cleveland together. Maybe this was the last day they'd spend together. Her nose burned and her eyes welled with tears. She didn't get it. Who WERE the Japs and why were they mad at them? And why did HER brother have to go fight them?

"Are you scared?" she asked as two men in glittery costumes shimmied up thick ropes to get to the trapeze overhead.

154

"Naw, not really." He swung the bag over one shoulder. "You set any bottles you find on the bleacher. I'll go empty this and come back."

"Why not?" She stuck her head out between two seats.

"I don't know." He shrugged. "Maybe cause it doesn't seem real yet."

"Yeah." That made sense to her. How can you be afraid of something so far away? She went back to work as he walked around the first ring to dump the bottles into the box across from the Big Top. A net swung gracefully under the trapeze where the flyers were practicing. That was good. It wasn't so scary with the net.

Suddenly there was a commotion outside the Big Top -- shouting, scuffling, and a shrill metallic screech. Danny was nowhere in sight. She got down on her stomach on the grass and slipped her head under the bottom of the tent. Someone's burning hot dogs, she thought. A canvas top shading Gargantua and his mate connected the Big Top with the Menagerie. The gorillas bounced up and down in their cage and pounded their chests in alarm. Their handlers cut the lines with an ax and the canvas top dropped over their cage. Two other men threw water on them.

Odd bits of smoldering straw and blackened paper drifted down between the tents. Pam looked up. The roof of the Menagerie was on fire. A zebra galloped by. His mouth was open and she could see his quivering tongue. A burning square of canvas drifted down on his back and he bucked and kicked, braying like a donkey. The gorilla cage blocked him in so he spun in a tight circle and headed back towards where he came.

Directly across from her, Bennie Bermeister crawled out from under the sidewall of the Menagerie. He looked left and right before standing up. She was right there in front of him but he didn't speak to her. He dusted the dirt off of the front of his uniform before strolling towards the lake whistling.

"You BASTARD!" She screamed after him. He glanced back and laughed, extending his middle finger, before squeezing past the gorillas and heading towards the railroad tracks.

She wiggled and pulled herself out from the tent as she'd seen Bennie do. The breeze off Lake Erie blew her long hair into her eyes. Flames crackled in the tent across from her. Elephants trumpeted, lions roared. Someone hooked the gorilla cage to a tractor and pulled it to safety. Where was Danny? She ran to the front of the Menagerie. Smoke curled around her as she crouched in the doorway -- stinging her eyes and covering her with a thick, waxy soot. Almost blind, she felt people run past her into the tent, others ran out with bawling, stamping animals on leashes. Heat seared her lungs.

An ostrich came at her, his feathers on fire. She ducked low and he bounded over her. Three men chased him down, wrestling the big bird to the ground and beating out the flames with their hands. His beak opened and closed slowly. All along his back and up his neck, his feathers were gone and the flesh beneath was bloody red. Pam knew instinctively he would die.

A giraffe raced out of the tent, its bulk looming over her. Pam turned and ran towards the ticket booth -- the big animal close behind. Tripping, she fell hard, hitting her mouth on a small rock. She covered her head with her hands and the giraffe stepped over her body before wandering down towards the mess tent across the road.

She sat up and touched her mouth. A piece of her front tooth dropped into her palm. Her lip bled profusely. She touched it with her tongue. A giant came out of the smoky chaos and she rolled out of his path. He ran into the burning Menagerie bellowing orders. Pam covered her mouth and nose with Danny's handkerchief. How could anyone run INTO that heat? A moment later, a line of elephants filed out, each one holding onto the tail of the one in front. Their ears were blackened. Strips of flesh hung from their sides and backs. One elephant refused to leave. As the burning tent began collapsing around her, the tall man who was obviously the elephant trainer finally ran for his life, the side of his face covered with bright pink blisters. The last elephant swayed from side to side and wailed as the flames enveloped her. The camels all burned -- and the cats in their cages.

A shriek pierced Pam's ears. It went on and on. Animals and people ran around her as she sat in the dust and still the screaming continued. A white-faced angel dashed towards her. He floated through the clouds of smoke and grabbed her roughly.

"Pammie, oh Pam." Danny picked her up like she was a baby. She wrapped her arms around his neck and her legs around his waist. It was then she realized the screams were her own.

The Menagerie was mostly gone now, nothing left but the poles. Circus water trucks and Cleveland fire engines arrived and sprayed water on the burning elephant. The stench overwhelmed them, and Pam gagged.

"Oh God, that's Ringling Rosie," a fireman yelled as he directed a stream towards the injured beast who stood bleeding amidst the charred cages of dying animals.

"Ringling Rosie?" Pam lifted her head.

"Are you hurt?" Danny rubbed the grime from her face with his thumbs. She jerked her face away from him, trying to look over his shoulder into what used to be the Menagerie. "Stop it now, tell me. Are you hurt?"

"Ringling Rosie?" Across the midway, the suffering elephant caught her eye. Pam stretched out her left hand to the beast who lifted her scorched trunk and trumpeted weakly.

Danny hugged Pam close to his body. "Let's get you out of here."

"NO! NOOOOOO!" She sobbed as he fought his way through the crowds of people congregating around the smoldering corpses. The big man was trying to chain Rosie so the veterinarian could treat her, but she swayed from side to side -- pulling away from him one moment, charging him the next.

"Do it, damnit. DO IT!" The giant cried and a shot rang out. Rosie fell, whimpering and squirming in the muddy ashes. Pam screamed without sound. After a moment, she closed her mouth slowly and laid her head in the crook of Danny's neck.

"It's not enough," the veterinarian yelled. "Get someone down here with something bigger."

"I-I have a submachine gun in the car," a youthful policeman said, his Adam's apple bobbing.

"Get it, Goddammit. Can't you see she's hurting?" The giant paced back and forth wringing his hands.

"I don't think I can do it."

The tall man grabbed the front of the policeman's shirt. "GET IT!" The young man ran back to where the police cars were parked.

"Can you walk?" Danny whispered into Pam's ear. She nodded and he sat her on her feet. "Hold my hand. Let's start walking towards East Ninth. If we can't get to the road, we'll climb up the embankment, okay?"

The young policeman hurried past them with a big gun in his hands. They passed the elephant conga line. The big animals were swinging their trunks and moaning while their handlers treated their burns. Pam stared in horror before looking away. They were several blocks from the Menagerie when they heard the submachine gun blast. Pam cried out and started running.

• • • • •

The train rocked as they made the first curve out of town. Danny put his arm around Pam. Her eyebrows and lashes were singed. Bits of scorched hair fell onto her lap and the shoulder of Danny's dirty white uniform. Soot and caked blood covered her face.

"I can't get that smell out of my nose." She hiccupped. "It makes me feel sick."

"I couldn't find you. What would I have told Pop if I'd lost you, if you'd been hurt or killed?" Danny rubbed at her face with the soiled handkerchief he'd given her hours earlier. "I don't think he could stand it, Pam. He's lost so much. I don't think he could stand losing you."

"I'm not lost." She hiccupped again. His eyes were red and his blonde hair was almost black from the smoky grit and ashes. "I'm fine. I'm not even burned."

"What were you trying to do? Save the damned animals?"

"You weren't around. I got scared and peeked under the wall of the Big Top when I heard the commotion. When I saw the Menagerie on fire, I thought I better get out of there." She remembered the whooshing roar of the flames and her sudden terror. "And then things just happened around me."

"You could have been trampled or run over." Danny shook his head and blew air through his lips. "I've got to leave tomorrow. I've got to take you home and tell Pop what happened and then leave."

"Danny, I saw Bennie. I think he started the fire." Pam wiped her nose on her sleeve. "He was in the Menagerie when it started."

"Oh, Pam. Bennie's a pain but he wouldn't do something like that." Danny was too good. He couldn't imagine someone he knew would do something bad. Pam admired him. She wasn't like that, but she admired him.

"I screamed at him and he grinned like he knew something no one else did. He didn't even try to help me out from under the tent. He just ran off. The BASTARD!" Pam had known tragedy before, but never evil of this magnitude.

"Why? Why would he do such a thing?" Danny shook his head again.

"Because he's mean. He's always been mean."

"He's only seventeen years old. He's a kid just like us."

"He's never been like us. He used to pull Taminee's tail. That's why she ran off whenever he came over. And I saw him kick the black rooster that time it turned up with a broken leg. For no reason. And he was always punching me when you weren't looking."

"That cat ran away whenever any of the guys came over, Pam. She didn't like the noise."

"Yeah, right." Pam folded her arms over her chest and pouted. "I saw him, Danny. I think we ought to tell someone. Call the Cleveland police when we get home, maybe."

"Did you see him light the fire?"

That brought her up short. "No, but I KNOW he did it."

"You don't know anything. You saw him leaving the tent. Everyone runs from fire, Goober. Everyone."

"I didn't."

"You should have."

"What about all those animals? The lions? That big bird? What about Ringling Rosie?" She would always remember the flames reflected in the little elephant's eyes.

"Just because it was awful doesn't mean it's anyone's fault."

"SOMEONE did it."

"It could have been an accident. Maybe it was an electrical spark or maybe a lantern exploded or maybe it just got too hot in there and something ignited. Bad stuff happens all the time without it being anyone's fault."

That idea scared her. If it was someone's fault, they could tell on them and the police would come and put them in jail and then everything would be safe and normal. The idea that catastrophe could be a bolt out of the blue -- as uncontrollable as a sneeze, that was just too much to accept. "It's not FAIR!" She wailed. Ringling Rosie had reached out to her in her final

160

agony, reached out to her to square things. "There has to be something we can do."

"What? Accuse Bennie? You can't prove it. What if you tell everyone and the police arrest him and he's punished? What if they put him in jail for a long time? And then you find out you were wrong? Think about his mama and daddy. Think about his little brother."

She scowled at him. "But someone has to pay for this. What if it IS Bennie and no one tells on him? What if he does it again? What if he burns someone's barn? Or someone's house?"

"That's a chance we have to take, isn't it?"

"It's not fair."

"Whoever said life was fair?" The corners of his mouth turned downwards.

"It's supposed to be." She sniffed. "It's supposed to be, Danny."

THE TEST

The old man stood over the crib with a butcher knife. The boy's copper curls reminded him of Sarah's forty years ago.

They had lost hope. Then, when it should have been too late -- when the lines on her lovely face deepened, after her breasts softened and drooped -- she conceived. He'd been incredulous, thrilled.

Shadows of carved wooden camels and elephants and giraffes flickered in the dusky lamplight. A music box plinked out a Mozart melody.

He hovered over the crib -- an indecisive wraith, lifting and lowering the blade. Smiling, the infant gripped the old man's index finger. Laying the knife on the nightstand, he picked up his son and cuddled him. "I can't do it," he whispered. "I won't."

"Where are you?" Sarah called from the kitchen.

He tucked the baby back into bed. Slipping the knife into his waistband, he hurried out of the nursery. She stood at the sink washing dishes. Creeping up behind her, he slipped his arms around her waist.

"Is he asleep?"

"Sawing logs," he said.

She turned to him and kissed his lips. They had renewed their love affair after years of estrangement. He blamed himself for those awful nights spent in different rooms. He focused on his career and a series of women who fluttered in and out of his life. One night he simply returned to her bed -- luxuriating in her familiar body and making promises he intended to keep. A few months later she was pregnant.

He was with her when she delivered. They were the most elderly first-time parents in the history of the hospital. Doctors and nurses eyed him over their multi-colored masks as he reached for his son and held the infant over his head in a spontaneous gesture of benediction and thanksgiving. Sarah prayed with him, joy choking her delicate soprano.

"I won't be gone too long." She returned to the dishes. "I'm going to see the doctor first and then I'm off to the Piggly Wiggly. I expressed two bottles of milk, just in case, but I doubt you'll need more than one."

"Don't worry. I'll take care of him." He poured a cup of coffee and sat down at the table, conscious of the knife hidden in his waistband.

She hung her bright red apron on a hook behind the door. "I've never seen you like this before."

"What do you mean?" His throat was dry. He took a quick sip of hot coffee.

"Happy." She sat in his lap. "You seemed far away -- like religion took up all of your energy and there was no room for me, but since the baby, you've been with me."

"I've always loved you, Sarah." He rubbed his face against her bosom inhaling her milky scent. She seemed light -- like her bones were hollow and he had to hold on to her or she'd drift away like a balloon.

She kissed his forehead. "I need to get going." He followed her down the hall and peeked in on the sleeping infant while she drew on her eyebrows and colored her lips.

"I want you to remember it, no matter what happens," he said as she got into her minivan a few minutes later.

"What do you think is going to happen?"

"Nothing."

"I'll be back soon, sweetheart." The minivan growled as she shifted into first gear.

Back in the living room, he turned on the TV. The Cardinals were playing on ESPN. "You know what you have to do," the announcer spoke directly to him. He switched to Court TV. "It's unclear what action the old man will take, but if he chooses to break the law, he will be prosecuted." He turned the television off and opened the newspaper.

"MAN MUST KILL NEWBORN TO PROVE LOVE!" The red-inked headline covered four columns. Acid seared his esophagus. His legs ached and his hands shook. He tossed the newspaper into a waste paper basket.

In the bathroom, he found a ragged copy of The Globe. "GOD CHALLENGES LONG TIME BELIEVER" danced across a picture of him and Sarah leaving the hospital with the baby. He ripped the cover off the magazine, tore it into strips and flushed it down the toilet.

Back at his desk, he checked his email. There were three messages from The Voice@aol.com. "Leave me alone," he muttered as he deleted without reading them. He was reviewing market quotes when an Instant Message popped up.

"Don't think you can duck me," The Voice wrote.

"Why this?" the old man responded. His fingers were stiff. "Haven't I followed all the rules? Did everything you asked?"

"Until now."

"It would break Sarah's heart. It would break mine."

"Priorities. You must think about priorities," The Voice answered.

He peered through the lower lens of his bifocals. "If you are who you say you are, why do you need proof?"

"Why do you question everything?"

"My job is to protect him. To teach him to take care of himself. To show him how to be a good person. How can you ask a father to kill his own child?"

"Trust me!" In a bold red font, the words marched across his screen. He turned off the computer and stood up, covering his face with his hands and breathing heavily. The flat of the blade pressed into the flesh of his back.

He gathered up his son, covering him with a sweater. The screen door bumped against his back as he hurried out, the child cradled against his heart. He headed towards Heavenly Hills, an estate down the road from their plan. Breaking through a hedge of red rhododendrons, he laid the infant on a blanket at the foot of a large oak tree. The boy cried out and kicked vigorously.

Staring up through the leafy branches, he prayed. "I can't do this, please don't make me do this." The sky was disappointingly silent, the leaves frozen silhouettes. "Please!" There was no answer.

He pulled the knife from his pants and grasping the hilt with both hands, raised it over his head -- the tip of the blade aimed at his tiny son's heart.

The old man stopped the knife's downward thrust eighteen inches from the child's chest when he heard the engine. A car parked at the curb just the other side of the rhododendrons. He sat back on his heels and waited, his head bowed -- hoping.

A tall black man in a white suit got out of the car smoking a cigar and holding a bottle of merlot. "What's going on back here, Abe?" He climbed through the hole in the hedge holding the cigar between his teeth.

"Michael. I was afraid you wouldn't come," the old man said as he dropped the knife. "I was afraid you'd be too late."

"I'm here for him as much as for you." Michael pointed at the bright-eyed baby. "I wouldn't let anything happen to him."

"I'd rather die myself."

"That was always an option." Michael tickled the baby and the boy cackled with delight.

"Good. Then let's do that." Relief washed over the old man. He had lived a good life. He'd made mistakes and been forgiven. He'd found Sarah again. How could anyone be more blessed? He'd gladly go in the baby's place. His future lay with this child anyway.

"You think it's that easy? You think you get to choose?" Michael sat down on the blanket and picked up the cooing baby. The infant smiled at Michael like he was an old friend.

"What then? What does He want?"

"Nothing. Now." Michael bounced the baby on his knee. "You passed."

"I passed?" Abe leaned back against the trunk of the tree, trembling. "You mean this was a test?" He folded his arms over his chest and put out his lower lip, his relief fading into anger. "He knew." He thumped his head against the trunk of the tree. "He knew I would obey and He knew you would come."

"Of course, He did," Michael said.

Covering his face with his hands, Abe shuddered as he realized how close it had been. "I thought I was crazy. Hearing things. What if you'd been late?"

"I wasn't." Michael blew smoke rings out of the corner of his mouth. They drifted in the stillness one floating through another until they dissipated.

"What if I had refused?"

"Well, that didn't happen either, now did it?" Michael gestured towards the merlot with his head. "Why don't you open up that wine?"

"Why?"

"To honor Him! To celebrate the birth of this miracle child." The baby's toothless grin matched Michael's broad one. "By the way, what's his name?"

"Isaac."

"What's wrong with Michael?" Michael puffed on the cigar, smoke encircling his head like a halo.

"His name is Isaac," the old man insisted.

"Well, don't get bent out of shape over it," Michael laughed. "He knows his Uncle Mike loves him, whatever his name. Isn't that right, little fella?" The baby giggled as Michael laid him back on the blanket.

The old man chewed his lip as he uncorked the wine. He was offended. Until he broke and came here to sacrifice his precious son, The Voice buzzed in his ears like the hum of a mosquito inside a tent. Now, there was only Michael -- and silence. "Do you have glasses?"

"KAZAM!" Michael pulled two paper cups out of his pockets. "I'm a boy scout too. Always prepared."

Abe poured into each cup. Giving one to the old man, Michael lifted the other towards the baby.

"To Isaac, may you have many children and grandchildren."

Abe frowned, but he took a cup and raised it towards the sky. "May he have a long and happy life," he said emphasizing the word 'long'.

"Amen." Michael picked up the butcher knife. "Think I'll take this with me. It's time I get on down the road. I got other folks to take care of this evening."

"Thank you, Michael," the old man said sourly.

"I'll be around." Michael crawled back through the hedges and got into the black car. "You keep the merlot. I got a cellar full back at the estate."

Abe nodded and waved.

Michael sped off down the road, dust curling behind him.

Holding Isaac to his shoulder, Abe started back. Home seemed to be a long way away. A half-block from the house, he heard the minivan growl behind them as Sarah downshifted into first.

"What are you doing out here with that baby?" She threw open the door and ran up to them, leaving the engine running.

"We went for a walk," he told her as she took Isaac into her arms. The baby whimpered when he recognized his mother, rooting around for her breast.

"It's hot as blue blazes out here, Abe. He's hungry! For crying out loud, can't I trust you to look out for this little guy?" She cuddled the infant.

Abe rocked on his heels, hiding the wine in the folds of the baby's blanket. He opened the passenger door and she crawled inside. It was only a few yards to their driveway, but he fastened her seatbelt anyway. He couldn't count on Michael for everything.

UNFORGIVABLE

At first it was just a vibration -- like a distant heartbeat, then the faint smell of smoke. Hedy opened her eyes. Someone stood at the foot of her bed.

"Mama?"

"I didn't mean to scare you." Alicia Jennings' cigarette glowed in the darkness.

"Why are you here? Is something wrong?" Hedy could just make out her mother's features in the gloom.

"You know why I came back."

"Tell him to leave me alone." Hedy pulled the quilt up under her chin.

"Comes a time when you have to let go of the past, Hedy. Forgive and forget -- that's what I say."

"I don't know how to do that." Hedy avoided Alicia's eyes. "I don't think I can."

"He's your father. You owe him."

"I do?"

"Don't take that tone with me, young lady."

Hedy sat up in bed. "How can you defend him after what he did to you? To us?"

"That was years ago -- he's paid for that."

"Maybe that's not up to you to say, Mama. You don't have to live with it every day."

Alicia stubbed out her cigarette in a china dish on Hedy's dresser. "He's changed."

"I hope so, for his sake."

"You are hard hearted, Hedy -- just like he used to be." Alicia lit another cigarette and exhaled.

"Don't do this to me, Mama." Hedy flinched. Smoke wasn't her favorite thing. "Mama?"

Alicia was gone.

"For God's sake, will this nightmare never end?" Every time her father's case came up for review, Alicia came to plead for him.

Something sparkled in the mirror. Hedy threw on her robe and got up. It was the reflection of her mother's lighter setting in the dresser. It was still warm.

Holding it against her cheek, she examined her own reflection. The shiny scar started below her right eye, snaked down her jaw, crossed her upper chest and sliced her forearm from elbow to wrist. Time and several surgeries had minimized the grotesquerie, but it was an ugly reminder of the things she learned at her father's knee.

Sleep was no longer an option even though it was only six-thirty in the morning. She sighed and dropped the lighter into her robe pocket. In the living room, she curled up in front of the television under a blanket. Clay Jennings's face flashed on the screen. The documentary on his case was on Court TV again. She clicked it off before they showed the famous photograph of Ronnie Kowalski carrying her out of the flames. Thirty-eight years since that night and it was still in her face.

• • • • •

She was kissing Ronnie Kowalski on the front porch swing when her father yelled from the back of the house, "YOU STUPID BITCH!"

170

Ronnie startled. "What the hell?"

She flushed. Couldn't she have one nice evening without them embarrassing her?

"STAY BACK!" A loud crash drowned out Alicia's voice.

"Should we do something?" Ronnie peered into the living room window. "Maybe they need help?"

"They're fine -- just drunk."

• • • • •

The doorbell woke her.

"Miz Jennings?" The white-suited man towered over her.

"What do you want?"

"I'm Gabriel Angelino?" His embossed business card included 'Esquire' after his name. "I represent Clay Jennings in his appeal?"

"There's nothing I can do, Mr. Angelino." She tried to close the door, but he blocked it with his briefcase.

"I need to talk with you, ma'am."

Irritated, she sighed and let him in. Usually she wore thick make-up, but she was in her nightclothes and her cheeks were clean. His eyes lingered on her scar. She resisted covering her face with her hand. Like he didn't know what happened. "Would you like a cup of tea?"

"Yes, ma'am. If you don't mind." He followed her into the kitchen and sat down at the table.

"Tell them that they can do anything they want. I don't care," she said as she put on the kettle.

"I'm afraid that's not good enough." He set his briefcase on the table. "He's not getting out until you forgive him. That's policy."

"I don't hate my father, Mr. Angelino. I'm not even mad at him. I moved on years ago. Okay?"

The lawyer took a file out of his briefcase. "It doesn't work that way. He's done his mandatory stretch, but now he has to get pardons from all the parties. Your mother indicated her willingness to forgive him years ago. You are the only one standing in his way."

• • • • •

Alicia's scream raised goose bumps on Hedy's neck.

"We need to help her," Ronnie stood up.

Hedy gripped his arm. "I'll go see what's going on."

"But what if she's hurt?"

"Go home, Ronnie." She gave him a push. "She won't want you in there."

He backed away. "What if you need me?" He called from the sidewalk.

"I won't." She turned and went inside.

• • • • •

Hedy poured hot water onto the tea bags inside each mug. "The state took care of all that right after it happened. It wasn't up to me then, I don't see why I have anything to say now."

Angelino held up a death warrant. "Your father paid his debt to the state twenty-nine years ago when he was executed."

"Closure." Hedy served his tea and sat down across from him. "That's what they said anyway -- but of course, whether he's alive or whether he's dead doesn't change anything for me."

"It was only the beginning for Mr. Jennings." Angelino handed her the record of her father's progress through the celestial courts. "As you can see, the clerk assigned him to me that same night. I presented his case a few days later and he moved to his current accommodations immediately after adjudication."

172

She rubbed her eyes. "So, is it like a prison for ghosts?"

"You are dealing with a whole other organization now, Miz Jennings. Different rules, different punishments, different opportunities."

• • • • •

The struggle in the kitchen escalated. Another crash. Scuffling. Screams, grunts and a strange gurgling sound. Heart pounding, Hedy burst through the door. Her mother writhed on the table trying to ward off the long butcher knife clutched in her father's hand.

"NO!" Hedy froze in the doorway. "Stop it, Daddy!"

The knife sliced through Alicia's fingers and hit the table beside her head. Something wet splattered Hedy's cheeks. Stunned, she wiped her face with the back of her hand. Blood!

Without thinking, Hedy tackled him screaming. "You're killing her, Daddy!"

"It's her own damned fault." Clay swung the knife in a wide arc, slashing Hedy's cheek. "She made me do it."

"Hedy," Alicia moaned, pink bubbles frothing from her nostrils. "Go get help."

"YOU STUPID BITCH." Clay Jennings lifted the knife over his head, aiming at Alicia's heart.

Hedy tried to push him away. "Don't you hurt my Mama!"

Clay flung her against the wall and she fell hard against an overturned chair. Her feet slipping on the bloody linoleum, she struggled to get up.

Alicia's scream was more of a wheeze. "Hedy, stay back --!"

Clay Jennings plunged the knife into Alicia's chest just as Hedy jumped between them.

• • • • •

"What happens next?"

"He'll be reassigned to a new body if everyone agrees that he's ready."

"Ready?" Hedy frowned.

"He's been through a lot."

"Has he?"

Angelino tapped the paper. "He's learned to accept responsibility for his choices. He understands that there are consequences even when a course of action is justified."

"Oh yes, it was our fault. We got in his way. We made him angry."

Gabriel Angelino raised an eyebrow.

She folded her arms across her chest. "You think I'm bitter, don't you?"

He shrugged.

"I'm not."

"Then why can't you forgive him?"

"I don't know how, Mr. Angelino. I don't even know what forgiveness is." She leaned her head on her hands.

"What do you think it is?" His voice was kind.

"At first, I thought it was letting go of the emotion. Moving on with my life. Not being angry -- but then that is about me. What good does that do him? He doesn't get a pass just because I'm doing okay."

Angelino's nod was noncommittal.

"Then I thought that it was about putting things right -- but there is no do-over here. My mother has been dead my whole adult life. I spent my twenties in hospitals -- first to fix my body, then to fix my mind. Then there were the trials, the appeals -- waiting for his execution. Getting over his execution." She sniffed. "He can't give me back my youth, Mr. Angelino -- or my mother."

174

"No, he can't." Angelino sighed.

"Someone once told me there was peace to be found in amnesia. I tried everything from meditation to hypnosis -- but how do I forget my mother's face that night? How do I forget that blade slicing into me? Or the smell of the blood? Do you know what it's like when someone you love wants you dead, Mr. Angelino?"

The tall man's eyes were damp.

She blew her nose on a paper napkin. "Actually, I don't want to forget. Those memories make me cautious -- wise."

"Wisdom comes at a price," Angelino agreed.

"And even if I DO forget, how does that help my father?"

"Has nothing to do with him, that's for sure."

• • • • •

The pain didn't start right away. She lay on the kitchen floor -- numb, bleeding. She thought she heard Alicia's last breath. Clay staggered around the room, sobbing. "Look what you made me do, you bitch." He slapped Alicia's cheeks, trying to revive her. "Don't you dare die on me."

Hedy gritted her teeth, hoping he would pass out before she did.

Dropping the knife, he dragged Alicia's body off the table and fell to the floor with it, cradling her in his arms. "Don't leave me, baby."

In the distance, a siren distracted him. Through half closed eyes, Hedy watched him. Drunk, distraught and frightened, he arranged Alicia on the floor beside him -- straightening her legs, smoothing back her hair. On all fours, he crouched over her -- wailing. "ALICIA!"

The siren grew louder. Clay Jennings quieted, listening. Wiping his nose on the back of his hand, he lumbered to his feet and looked around. The evening newspaper was on the table, Alicia's last cigarette smoldering in the ash tray beside it. He wadded up the top sheet -- then the second one.

Using the cigarette butt, he lit sheet after sheet and tossed them around the room until the thin curtains over the sink ignited. Still sobbing, he lay down beside Alicia.

Smoke filled the room quickly. Hedy closed her eyes, knowing that she was going to die soon. She felt the heat on her face and heard the flames crackling. Her father coughed. She opened her eyes. He got to his feet and stumbled out the back door, gasping for breath.

"Bastard," she thought.

• • • • •

Angelino laid a thin white envelope on the table in front of her.

Hedy wiped her eyes. "What happens if he gets a new body? Will I have to spend the rest of my life looking over my shoulder?"

"He wouldn't do that."

She bit her lip. "What's to stop him?"

"Well, he'll be a baby for one thing. Not much chance he'll come track you down for many years to come."

"Is that supposed to comfort me?"

"He won't remember the incident after he moves on to his new family. Only the psychic growth from his years in purgatory will remain."

"So he gets to forget?"

"He's been punished -- twice."

"When do I get paroled, Mr. Angelino? When do I get to sleep through the night without thinking about what he did to my mother? When do my scars go away?"

"I have no answers for you, Miz Jennings." He pointed to the envelope in front of her. "You'll do what you do. It's no skin off my nose either way."

She ran her finger across the surface of the letter. "What do I have to do? Sign a paper?"

Angelino grunted. "I hardly think that your signature means much one way or another. It's what's in your heart that matters."

"Should I open it?"

He shrugged.

Trembling, she picked up the letter. She never spoke to her father after that horrible night. He never tried to contact her either -- not while he was on death row and, unlike Alicia, no ghostly visits since. She wasn't sure she wanted to know what he had to say for himself. She wasn't sure she could bear it.

A single piece of paper was inside the envelope.

"HEDY." Clay Jennings never wrote in cursive -- only thick, primitive printing. She didn't doubt the note was from him.

"I FACE AN ETERNITY OF SUFFERING. ONLY YOU CAN GIVE ME ANOTHER CHANCE. HAVE MERCY ON ME, DAUGHTER."

She looked up at Gabriel Angelino. "It's not much, is it?"

"It took him a lifetime to write that."

"Yes, he's very proud."

"Sometimes you have to consider what a person has to give." Angelino's voice was soft. "A half-empty container is empty long before a full one."

A sob caught in her throat like a hiccup. "And you expect more of me, Mr. Angelino?"

"I think you expect more of yourself."

"Ronnie Kowalski broke into that burning house to save me. He beat the flames out of my clothes with his bare hands. He was with me every day during my recovery. His scars are as deep as mine -- and try as I might, I can't squeeze out one ounce of affection for him." She held up the letter. "But this crazy son of a bitch who thinks he can reach into my heart and crush it whenever he wants, I adore. It doesn't seem fair."

"Sometimes there are no good choices, Hedy -- only a bunch of bad ones."

She stiffened. It was the first time Angelino had used her given name. "And no matter what I choose, there will be a penalty."

"Yes -- and a reward."

She dug Alicia's lighter out of the pocket of her robe. "Some rewards aren't worth the pain, Mr. Angelino." She held her father's letter over the flame.

"What shall I tell him?" The tall man closed his briefcase and stood up.

"Tell him that I understand -- and that I'm sorry."

Voices (9/11)

•• Ginger ••

Nikki lost her shoe on the eighty-first floor. "Keep going," I told her. "It's just a shoe."

A heavy-set woman wobbled in front of us. I reached out to steady her. She whirled on me and screamed. "What are you? In a hurry?"

"Well, excuse me!" We squeezed around her. "Bitch!" I muttered under my breath.

"She's scared." Nikki whispered in my ear.

"Everyone's scared."

"We'll be okay. There's nothing wrong with this building. You'll see."

I wasn't so sure. The sight of the plane hitting the other tower still burned in my retinas. I had been afraid the fireball was going to reach our building. It got so hot that papers on my desk scorched. When my boss came around telling us to leave, I was still sitting there -- staring out the window at what was happening to the people across the way.

I shuddered and tried to push that thought out of my mind as we clumped down the stairs. Getting out was all that mattered now. My knees ached. I gritted my teeth -- one step at a time. Keep going.

We were on the twenty-seventh floor when the announcer told us to return to our offices. Yeah. Right. No way was I going back up.

Nikki turned around. "I'm going after my shoe."

"NO!" I reached for her hand.

She laughed. "Chill. It's Armani. I'll be in the office when you get through milling around on the sidewalk."

•• Farah ••

I was in the lab when the planes hit the towers. I heard the hubbub and came out into the corridor. People stood around a television in one of the waiting rooms, arms crossed over their chests. I covered my mouth with both hands as I saw the buildings burning in New York. I prayed that the hijackers were not from my country. I prayed for the people dying before my eyes.

The air conditioning was too high. I rubbed my arms, trying to warm them. It seemed like a disaster movie -- The Towering Inferno. Techs gathered around the coffee pot, their voices subdued. When they announced that still another plane had crashed into the Pentagon, everyone gasped. A colleague ran to the window and pressed his face against the glass. I caught an old friend staring at me with a frown on his face. People ran up and down the halls with cell phones in their fists.

I went back to the lab and called my husband's office. I called several times before he answered. "One of the towers fell." His voice rasped like dry leaves. "If the terrorists' don't kill us, our neighbors will." It broke my heart. His mother was born in Georgia. He graduated from Georgia Tech. He is as American as anyone, but I knew he was right. Scared people don't know a Sikh from a Sheik or a fellow citizen from a lunatic in a turban.

I told him I'd pick up the children and meet him at home. I hung my smock in my locker and grabbed my purse -- praying that no one would stop me as I hurried out to my car.

180

Frightened faces pretended they weren't watching me as I folded the sunscreen and put it in the trunk. It was only mid-morning, but traffic clogged the streets.

My children sat on the doorstep, put out by their angry blonde babysitter. The older one burst into tears when he saw me. The baby didn't understand and played happily with a toy airplane. The neighbors watched me tuck them into their car seats. My hands were trembling. My Muslim rosary dangled from the rear view mirror. I unwound it and put it in my lap. I drove through the tree-lined streets of Atlanta, hoping that the people on the corners would think we were Hispanic.

The uniformed guard that had waved and smiled when I left our gated community this morning glared at me as I drove past. As I turned into the driveway, I saw my husband on the balcony hanging the stars and stripes over our door.

"Daddy, Daddy!" Our son rolled down the window and waved.

My husband spun around holding a finger over his lips. I drove into the garage and lowered the door behind me.

•• Everet ••

When I saw the towers come down on CNN, I felt it like a stab in the gut. "How dare they? HOW DARE THEY! Who would do this? I want them dead. No. I want them to suffer first. If I wasn't an old man, I'd kill them myself. This is MY country." I cleaned my guns and propped them up behind the door so I could get to them if they came for me. I counted the boxes of shells. Not enough. Not near enough. While the dust was still settling in New York, I drove down to the Wal-Mart and emptied my checking account buying shells and powdered milk and canned goods and Snickers bars and gallons and gallons of water. Back at the house, I settled in to wait. "Just try it, asshole. I'm here. Waiting."

•• Ione ••

"Which flight?" I rummaged through the papers on his desk. "Which one?" I tried his cell phone again. This number is out of range. "Where the hell is he? Okay, calm down. He always flies United. Doesn't he?" I couldn't remember. "Okay, relax. What airports did they say?" The TV was blaring. "Come on, tell me. Tell me. What airports?" I changed channels. The plane hit the tower again and again in rerun hell. "No, it's not his plane. No. I won't believe it." I hit redial. "Oh Danny! Call me, call me. Don't be dead, Danny. Call me."

•• Ronald and Charlie ••

I called the station to volunteer. The captain said to wait until they worked something out. Surely they were going to need help up there. It wasn't quite eight hours away. No matter what the captain said, I was going. I went down the back steps and called to Charlie. "Here, boy!" I patted my chest. He nearly knocked me over in his enthusiasm, putting his paws on my shoulders and licking my face. "We got work to do, buddy." I clipped the leash to his harness. It was such a beautiful day.

•• Bobby ••

"Are they going to hit our house, Mommy?" She held me too tight and I couldn't breathe. "Are the bad men coming to Paducah too?" She told me no, but I didn't believe her. Lunch was yucky. I hid my sandwich in my back pocket. She wouldn't let me watch TV so I played Game Boy all afternoon. I heard her calling Daddy, even though they didn't' like each other anymore. I was glad they didn't yell but it scared me too. Grandma came by with lots of groceries. None of the kids got to go out that day. I didn't want to anyway. I curled up behind the green chair and fell asleep trying not to suck my thumb.

•• Gilbert ••

I'm an American. I've been in uniform four years, waiting for the chance to prove myself. My heroes have always been soldiers -- Old Blood n Guts, Stormin Norman and my uncle

Doug who won a silver star in Vietnam. I want to be like them -- someone to be counted on, someone who counts. I missed the last war, but I'm here now. Trained. Ready to go. This is my chance to kick some butt -- to make my mother proud of me. Tell me what to do. Where to go. Hooah! I'm ready to die, but am I ready to kill? I thought I was. This is real, not a fantasy. Oh God! Don't let me mess up. Don't let anyone see that I'm afraid.

•• Sheila ••

My crutches clunked against the porch as I hobbled back and forth. "I knew it! I knew this would happen when they stole the election. There's no one to protect us now. The worst thing that's ever happened to us and we can't trust the guys in charge."

Armando wheezed. He's close to eight hundred pounds and has asthma. Talking's hard for him.

"You think they'll hit Cleveland too?"

He shook his head and struggled to breathe.

I leaned over the railing and scanned the sky for anything suspicious. "How could they hijack FOUR planes? Someone had to have looked the other way. What if there are more out there? What if they hijack trucks? Or buses?"

Armando's breathing suddenly became a thin whistle. He opened his mouth trying to force air in and out of his lungs, his eyes wide with fear.

"Damnit, Armando. Don't you do this to me." I turned to call the nurse, lost my balance and nearly fell into the rose bushes. What are people like us supposed to do? We can't run. We're sitting ducks for anyone that wants to do us in. "GET SOME HELP OUT HERE!" I yelled through the screen door. "Armando's choking to death."

Two big nurses came running out with Armando's machine.

An aide came for me. I'd never seen her before. Maybe she was one of THEM. I backed away. "Where's the Air Force? Where's the president? I KNEW I couldn't count on the government."

"Shush," she said as she took away my crutches and got me into a chair. "No sense getting yourself all worked up."

"Armando!" I screamed as she wheeled me back into the center.

•• Rachel ••

All I wanted was to live in peace. After Auschwitz, I need safety. Quiet. Food. My parents are ashes. My three sisters. Right after the war, I emigrate to Israel and marry -- but the Arabs hate us. They hate us so much. They want to push us into the sea. I was weary of hatred even before the explosion that killed my Jakob, so I come to Chicago America where I can start once again with a new husband and a new family. It took fifty years, but the poison followed me here. I can't bear it to happen again. I'm tired. I think maybe it's time I rest. Maybe forever.

•• Bull ••

I was at the gym, pressing two-fifty, when one of the guys turned up the sound on the television. I dropped the weight and focused on the huge cloud of dust rushing toward the cameraman. "What the hell?" I never seen anything like it. Then the word that people jumped from those buildings before they buckled. Firemen were killed, they said. Rescue workers? It was too much to take in all at once. I picked up a soy drink and straddled the bench, watching one of the half dozen monitors positioned around the room. When you stopped working out, you picked up a chill pretty quick, but I couldn't make myself leave. "Day-um!" Even perky Katie Couric looked shocked and pale. Where was my man? Where was Dubya? He'd swoop in like superman and find the bastards that done this and extract some Texas justice and everything would be okay again.

•• Luci Ann ••

I didn't care. I didn't know anyone in New York or DC. None of my friends would be caught dead on an airplane. Pennsylvania was half a continent away. The damned TV gave me a migraine so I turned it off. The desert sun baked our stucco house even though it was still early morning. I turned the air conditioner on full blast. The cold air was refreshing. I closed the blinds and locked the backdoor. It was a good thing I had re-filled my prescription while in town. I took two Valium and lay on the couch, covering my face with a quilt. "I don't care," I murmured before falling asleep. "I don't."

•• Barkley ••

"Hold me," I said to her when I got home. The dust covered me from head to toe. It was in my hair and it clung to my eyelashes. The stench of wickedness lingered in my clothes. It mattered so much to me that it didn't matter to her. She held me while I cried -- great coughing sobs. I stopped when I couldn't go on any more, but not crying was worse. I could see things in my mind's eye that I'd rather not remember. She held out her hand and led me into the shower -- unbuttoning my shirt while I watched a slack-faced stranger in the mirror. I lifted one foot and then the other as she untied my oxfords and peeled off my socks. The hot water hit my flesh like molten pins. I stared at the showerhead, my mouth agape. She slipped in beside me, naked. With a soapy cloth, she scrubbed me down -- paying special attention to the creases in my neck, behind my ears, between my fingers and toes. Using baby shampoo, she washed my hair three times, the suds draining down over my shoulders. Then, she rubbed me with a thick towel until the rosy pink color returned to my skin, kissing between my shoulder blades and the palms of my hands. I concentrated on not thinking while she put me to bed. The linens smelled of Downey. I laid my cheek on the pillow and she slid in behind me, wrapping her arms around my waist. "Thank God you are safe," she whispered into my ear before she let herself cry. I stared at the wall, unblinking.

WINDING DOWN

The flight to Dallas took three hours. I sat alone at the gate waiting for the shuttle to Fort Smith.

"Is something wrong?" A heavy-set man stood in front of me, his overcoat looped over one arm, the strap of his bulging briefcase hooked over the other.

"A family emergency."

"Someone sick?" He sat down across from me.

I recognized his aftershave. He sat behind me on the plane from Cleveland. "My mother."

"Is there anything I can do to help?"

What the hell did he think he could do? Save her? "I don't think so."

"I have a cell phone you could use."

"I couldn't."

"The company pays for it. Go ahead." He handed it to me and sat back in the plastic bucket seat.

I stared at the phone for a moment before calling the hospital. Mrs. Zimmer was in critical condition. At least she was alive. "Thank you." I handed the phone back.

"Is your father still alive?"

"No, he died a long time ago." I was annoyed with his questions, but talking was better than thinking.

186

"Are you close to your mother?" He slipped a cigar out of the inside breast pocket of his blazer and held it under his nose.

"No, I wouldn't say we are close. I love her, but we aren't close."

"Ahhhh." It was a soft breathy sigh.

"It's hard to explain."

"Yes, I imagine it is. Would you like something to eat?"

"I don't think I can keep anything down."

"Maybe a coke with lots of ice? That will settle your stomach sometimes." He didn't wait for my answer, but got up and disappeared down the hall, leaving all of his things on the chair across from me -- even his cell phone. The sheer lunacy of leaving expensive items with a complete stranger in an airport shocked me.

He returned with a cup full of Coca Cola. It was too sugary. I preferred diet cokes, but it was nice of him to get it for me. I realized I was thirsty once I took the first sip.

"I brought you a snack, too." He slipped a Snickers Bar into the side pocket of my purse. "Save it for when you need it."

"I can't tell you how much I appreciate all of this." I started.

"We all have mothers." He gathered up his stuff and walked away.

The plane reached Fort Smith twenty minutes later than scheduled. It was cool, but not cold. January in Fort Smith was a lot different than January in Cleveland. My baby sister was standing on the other side of the fence. Of course, she wasn't much of a baby anymore. She was twenty-seven years old. I left home when she was two. I didn't know her very well, and she certainly didn't know me. She looked like both of our parents. Her face, her bone structure was Mother's, but there was something about her eyes that reminded me of Daddy. I thought she was utterly beautiful.

"Hope, Hope!" She called. I waved and ran to hug her.

"How are you doing, Kitty?" I gave her that name. She was born prematurely and her cries were like the soft mews of a kitten.

"I'm fine."

"How's mother?"

"She'll be okay." She led me towards the tiny baggage claim department.

Her cheery, relaxed attitude puzzled me after our other sister's frantic phone call. "I hope so." We collected my luggage and hurried out into the parking lot where Kitty's tiny blue Chevette sat.

"Are you hungry? Do you want to go to the house first?"

The idea of going back to that house froze my heart. That was the LAST place I wanted to go. "No, I want to see Mother -- and I'd like to talk with the doctors."

"She likes her doctor." Kitty glared at me as she started the car.

"Oh?"

"I don't think we ought to talk with them behind her back."

"Oh?" The anger in her voice puzzled me. "What's up?"

"She's a private person. She doesn't like having everyone know her business."

"Kitty, we are her daughters. Don't we have a right to know what's happening with her?"

"If she wanted us to know, she'd tell us." She put the car in gear as if we had decided something.

I hadn't been back to Fort Smith in a long time. Trees were taller, a new freeway looped around the city, and old buildings were gone, replaced with shopping centers. Even the hospital was new and improved. Kitty parked in the back lot.

We went to the waiting room first. Our whole extended family was there. They crowded around me. My other sister Garnet found me, tears in her eyes, and held me close.

"It's bad, Hope."

My heart dropped. "What's happened?"

Garnet's eyes were full of grief. "You need to talk with the cardiologist."

Something about her voice made me ask, "Should I see him before we go see Mother?"

"He's waiting to talk with you."

Kitty folded her arms across her chest.

"You don't have to come with us, Kitty." Garnet said, "But I think it might be a good idea."

"She doesn't want us to do this." Kitty frowned.

"Okay, then Hope and I will talk to him without you."

"Won't you come with us, Kitty?" I touched her bicep. She jerked away, her eyes blazing.

"I have to go feed Tigger. No one's been out there all day. He's probably scared."

I was bewildered by her hostility. "Who's Tigger?"

"Mama's cat." Kitty took off down the hall twirling her keys. "I'll be back in an hour or so."

I turned to Garnet. "Who burnt her toast?"

"I don't know, Mama's sick, I guess." Garnet shrugged.

"She told me Mother was going to be fine."

"Well, she's not."

"Let's go talk with the doctor." I turned toward the Cardiac Intensive Care Unit.

"Just one thing, Hope. She's sick now. I don't want you upsetting her." Garnet avoided my eyes.

"There's nothing I can do about that. She upsets herself."

"I don't want any arguments."

"That's not anything anyone can control." I swallowed my irritation as we headed down the hall. I hadn't even been there five minutes, and it was starting. "Let's go find out what's happening here."

"We are here to see Dr. Frank. My sister just got in from Cleveland. The doctor was waiting to talk with her." Garnet said to the nurse at the central station. Monitors showing the heart rates of the various patients lined the wall. I wondered which one was for mother.

"I'll page him. Why don't you sit down over there?" She gestured to a couple of chairs against the wall. We sat down.

"So what happened this morning?"

"She had a heart attack -- and it was not her first. She's been sick for a long time they say."

I was aghast. "I spoke to her on the phone several times over the last few months and she never let on a thing."

"I knew she wasn't feeling well, but I thought it was her leg. She hasn't been able to walk without a cane in a while."

"She's only sixty-two years old. What did she need a cane for?"

"I don't know. She's had this pain for months. She couldn't sleep. Spent night after night in a chair because she couldn't stand laying down."

"Did she go to the doctor?"

"Oh yes, she loves her doctor." Garnet repeated Kitty's words with a hint of sarcasm.

"Mrs. Weaver, this is Dr. Frank, Mrs. Zimmer's cardiologist," the nurse said.

"Hope, I'm going to leave you with Dr. Frank. I'm going to go in and chat with Mother for a bit."

I looked at Garnet in surprise. She slipped her sweater over her shoulders and headed down the hall, disappearing behind one of the doors. What was THAT all about, I wondered.

Dr. Frank leaned against the nurses' station, doodling on an unlined pad. His face was serious. "Mrs. Weaver, I told all this to your sister, Mrs. Hunter, but she wanted me to tell you personally."

"Have you spoken with both of my sisters?"

"Yes, although I'm not sure Miss Zimmer fully appreciates the situation."

"What IS the situation?"

"Your mother has been sick for a long time."

"Has she been coming to you?"

"Not until she was admitted here last week."

Who WAS the doctor Mother loved so much? "What's the diagnosis?"

"Congestive Heart Failure. Over sixty percent of her heart is no longer functioning. There's not enough live muscle to pump blood throughout her body."

I digested this slowly. "So what can we do about it?"

"Not much."

"You mean there's nothing that can help her?" I was horrified.

"If she'd come to me sooner, we might have had a chance. It's too late now. The only thing that might help is a transplant and to be honest, Mrs. Zimmer would not survive that kind of operation. Besides, she isn't a good candidate. She is over sixty, she has diabetes and high blood pressure. Over the years, she had many different illnesses that have impacted her overall resilience."

"So you are telling me there's no hope?"

"There's no hope." His dark eyes met mine.

"God."

"You need to make a decision, Mrs. Weaver."

I was dizzy. "What decision is that?"

"If she were my mother, I'd let her go when she's called."

"Let her go?" I didn't understand what I could do about it.

"I'd leave an order not to resuscitate."

"What did mother say?"

"Your mother doesn't know."

"What?" I was surprised and outraged. "Why not? Isn't this a decision for her to make?"

"It's too late for that too." Dr. Frank sighed. "Her condition is so fragile that telling her about this could cause the final episode."

"It could kill her to ask her?"

"Yes."

"Does she know she's dying?"

"She may have guessed, but I doubt it."

"Kitty is telling her and everyone else she's going to get better, Dr. Frank."

"That's simply not the case."

I appreciated his bluntness. "What happens if we don't leave an order?"

"The hospital will have to use any means to try and bring her back. Shock, beating on her chest, and so forth. It could go on for days."

"If they bring her back, will she have good days?" I was willing to bargain for time.

"I doubt it. As more and more heart muscle dies, her circulation will get worse. That could lead to all kinds of things -- all of them bad, most painful. Now, I'm going to have to go.

You talk with your sisters and decide what you are going to do. I'll be back in the morning and we can chat again."

He held my hand for a moment in a sympathetic kind of handshake. His kindness choked me up. Then he left. I looked at the nurse standing behind the desk.

"I don't envy you this decision," she said.

"What would you do?"

"If you sign a 'no code blue' order, do you have the guts to sit there and hold her hand when she goes?"

I looked at her in surprise. "I have to have the guts to do that no matter what I decide."

She blinked. "Yes, no matter what you decide."

I was losing the battle with my emotions and my chin quivered. "What will happen when she goes?"

"She'll probably just pass out and stop breathing."

"She could go without ever knowing she's dying?" I thought about what that meant. It was all so unfair. Unfair that she was dying. Unfair that I had to decide anything. Unfair that she didn't know.

"Very possibly." She handed me a tissue and I blew my nose.

I paced up and down the hall, thinking. I had no idea what she would want. The things she wanted and the things I wanted had historically been very different. Kitty was denying mother was sick enough to die, but Garnet knew Mother better than I did. I'd see what she thought.

Composing my face, I took a breath and walked into Mother's room. "Well, here you all are!" I said cheerily. The ICU was cold. The air conditioning was running full blast and there was a small fan positioned so it blew directly on the patient. Garnet sat on a chair next to the bed, wrapped in a thick white sweater.

Mother was propped at an angle, her arms bruised by old and current punctures. The heart monitor left slow zigzagging electronic traces on a screen mounted on a tripod over her bed. An automatic blood pressure cuff encased one elbow and a tube snaked out from under the sheets, slowly filling a plastic bag with pale urine. She was beautiful -- her face unlined, her hair freshly dyed and coiffed. Even though she seemed weak, her eyes sparkled when she saw me. "It was a tough day, but I think the worst is over now."

"They taking good care of you, are they?" I kissed her on the forehead, gooseflesh rising on my arms.

"They are nice here, Hope. I know a lot of the nurses."

"That's cause you know everyone in Fort Smith."

"When I get out of here, I'm going to send them all thank you notes for being so kind." Mother was mindful of the rules of polite society.

"That would be lovely. How can you stand it being so cold in here?" I lifted my collar and folded my arms across my chest.

"Oh girl, when I first came in here, it was so hot I couldn't breathe. I'm comfortable now."

"Another degree or two and we'll see our own breath." I laughed because I didn't know what else to do. "You always did like living in a freezer."

"Never could stand hot weather," she agreed. "I complained until they brought me that dinky little fan. It helps some."

I glanced over at Garnet's troubled eyes. We shared the secret now. Our family had closets full of secrets. Was I the only one that hated them?

"Where you planning on staying, Hope?" Mother sipped iced water through a flexible straw stuck in a sweating cup.

"I thought I'd stay here with you if that's okay. I brought my things with me."

"I'd like that, maybe we can catch up."

"You had anything to eat yet?" Garnet asked me.

"No."

"Why don't we go get something to eat while Mama's got company? Aunt Betty is waiting to see her -- and Aunt Leigh. We can come back when everyone else is gone. Is that okay with you, Mama?" Garnet took my arm.

"You are going to stay awhile, Hope?" Mother seemed anxious.

"I'm going to stay until you are all better."

She smiled. "Great. If I'd have known it took getting sick to get you down here, I'd have gotten sick sooner." It struck me how big the lies got when someone was sick. Mother was always glad to see me come and equally glad to see me go. Who was she kidding?

Garnet and I walked down the hallway to the elevator and pushed the button. "She looks fine, doesn't she?" She rubbed her hands together to warm them. She was cold natured anyway. I was sure Mother's glacial hospital room was torture for her.

"I'm still stunned."

"What do you think we should do?" Garnet led the way to the cafeteria.

"It sounds like Kitty's not ready for this," I said.

"No, any decision that's made, we'll have to do it without her." Garnet picked up a tray and slid it along chrome rails in front of banks of fruit, cakes, pies, sandwiches and other saran-wrapped foods.

"You think Mother understands what's happening to her?"

"If she does, she's hiding it."

"Do you think she would want to know?" I picked out a carton of skim milk and set it on my tray. I was hungry but I wasn't sure I could eat anything.

"Would you?" Garnet turned to me with huge questioning eyes.

"Absolutely. It bothers me we can't tell her. It's like lying to her. How can we tell them not to resuscitate when we don't have a clue as to what she would want?"

Garnet shook her head as I paid for our food. We found a small corner table and sat down under the florescent lights. She played with her salad.

"You were with her a lot more than me, Garnet. Did she ever give you any indication as to what her feelings about this kind of thing are?"

"She never said anything."

"What if she has things she'd like to do before she dies? Maybe she would like to talk to someone, or say goodbye to her friends. Maybe she'd like to, I don't know -- talk with a minister of some kind? Do we deny her that?"

"How do you feel about the code blue?" Garnet asked.

"To me, that's easier. If Mother can't ever walk out of here alive, why should we torture her? The nurse said that when she goes, she will lose consciousness and stop breathing. That doesn't sound too bad. The idea of her being scared or hurting is a much uglier thought. It would probably get worse and worse for her each time they resuscitate. She would die in pieces. I'd rather just let her go when God calls." I sipped my milk.

"I don't know if I can decide." Garnet sighed.

"You'll be able to do what you have to." I smiled at her. It was the first piece of sisterly advice I could ever remember giving her. "We'll do it together."

"You decide and I'll back you," she said after a moment. "I'd rather do it that way."

196

I nodded. I didn't blame her. I was the oldest. Even though I hadn't been a part of the family for a long time, it was my responsibility.

The next morning I signed a paper requesting a "NO CODE BLUE" status. Kitty threw a fit when she heard.

"We should fight for life." She yelled, tears running down her cheeks.

"It will be easier on her. She's going to die, no matter what we do. This way, we let God make the decision." It had been agonizing. I sat beside Mother's bed watching her sleep most of the night. In the end, no one else wanted to decide so I did.

"How can you stand there and let your own mother die?" Her words were brutal, her face contorted.

"I can't help it, Kitty."

"You don't care. She's my mother and I don't want her to die."

"I don't want that either, but she's going to die regardless of what we want."

"She's MY mother."

Her sorrow pierced my heart. "You poor little thing."

"DON'T YOU EVER TALK TO ME LIKE THAT!" She took two steps towards me, her fists clenched, a vein in her forehead throbbing. "You don't even LIVE here. You left us a long time ago. Who are YOU to talk to me like that?"

I took the blow without wincing, but a tear ran down my cheek. She was right. I didn't live here. I turned away from her grief. I couldn't stand it.

"Kitty, you can't go on like this." Garnet said. "Pull yourself together. We have to be calm in front of Mama."

"You pull YOUR self together." She marched off down the hall towards the entrance, the heels of her shoes clicking on the tile floor.

Once she was gone, I leaned against the wall and sobbed for a moment. Garnet handed me a tissue from her purse. "Well, THAT was a catastrophe," I said after I blew my nose.

"She's upset."

"I understand, but what do we do to help her?"

"Leave her alone."

•••••

Now that I'd made the decision, Mother got better. She sat up in bed and chatted with us. She called her friends on the phone. She had visitors throughout the day. She looked happy. I wondered if we were getting a reprieve, if the gods had given us time. I also wondered if somehow Mother knew more than she was letting on.

Kitty breezed in with news from the college where mother worked and entertained her with the latest gossip. I was fascinated. I never remembered my mother gossiping. Mother never went anywhere or did anything when I was a child. Now it was clear that she went lots of places and did lots of things. I was happy for her. Garnet and Kitty had a much different relationship with our mother than I did. I was happy for them as well.

Mother had had so many drugs that she couldn't read, and she missed it. She didn't seem like herself without a book in her hand. I went down to the gift shop and bought a small tape player with headphones and a couple of taped novels. When visiting hours were over, she lay with the earphones on listening to her stories while I sat beside her, reading mine. At night, Garnet and I took turns, bundled up in jackets and sweaters, watching over her while she slept under a thin sheet.

Two days later, Mother and Garnet were chatting when I walked into her room. Someone had pulled the blinds and the afternoon sun was defeated. The relentless fan spun cold breezes. I shivered and put my hands in my pockets. The automatic blood pressure cuff inflated, took a read, deflated. I glanced at the heart monitor to see the read. The neat electronic shapes that had marched across the screen for the last few days were different now. Every third or fourth beat, the precise sharp tracing turned into a billowing cloud. Weird. I turned toward Mother's fan. The spinning blade was struggling. It would slow and then speed up. I wondered if something was wrong with the power.

Mother chuckled at something Garnet said.

A strange nurse came into the room and laid some clear plastic tubing on the food tray. "Would you girls step out for a minute? I need to change Mrs. Zimmer's tubes."

"We'll be right outside, Mama." Garnet leaned down to kiss her.

"Yell if you need us," I said.

"Maybe I'll try on that new gown when you get back." Mother fluttered her fingers to wave bye-bye.

Garnet and I sauntered down the hall. As we turned into the waiting room, we heard a persistent beeping sound and someone shouting, "Code Blue."

"There were two of those last night." I said to Garnet.

"I can't help but jump when I hear them." She took off her heavy sweater as the hallway warmed us. "I don't think I'll ever get used to them."

We sat down in the waiting room, chatting about this and that.

"Would the two of you please follow me?" A sober looking nurse said from the doorway.

Garnet and I looked at each other.

"Is something wrong?" My mouth was dry.

"Just come with me, please."

We stood up -- grabbing for each other's hand and followed the nurse into a private waiting room.

"Mrs. Zimmer has gone." The nurse lowered her eyes.

"GONE? Gone where?" Garnet's voice was over-loud in my ears.

"She's passed."

"We were just there." Garnet sat down on the couch, her hands over her eyes. "She was fine."

"How can she be dead?" I had no air. I had to force out the word "dead." Surely, this wasn't it? How could it all end, just like that? The petty family arguments, the secrets, the ancient resentments -- all of it gone in the blink of an eye? The door opened and one of our Zimmer cousins guided Kitty into the room. She was smiling, looking puzzled. Her eyes froze when she saw us.

"No, No! Don't YOU say anything!" She pointed at me. I pressed my back against the wall, my hands over my mouth, waiting for my mind to absorb the news.

Kitty accepted Garnet's hug, but not the news. "NOOOOOO." She wailed, holding her hands over her ears. "Not MY mother. Don't you tell me ANYTHING about my mother."

"Listen to me, Mama's gone." Garnet held Kitty's face with both hands.

Kitty's legs gave out. Garnet and I eased her to the floor in front of the couch. She sat cross-legged on the carpet. I felt her cries in the pit of my stomach. I cried for Kitty and for Garnet and for my mother. The nurse stood by the door, her head bowed. There was a knock on the door and she answered it for us. She leaned out -- talking with someone in the hall. Then she stepped out and closed the door behind her. I was thankful she was there to run interference. None of us were capable of talking. Not even to each other. I knelt down and hugged both of my sisters.

"Mrs. Weaver. Mrs. WEAVER." I looked up, tears streaming down my cheeks. The nurse stood in the open doorway looking at us with sympathy. She gestured to me and I stood up, leaving Garnet to console Kitty.

"Yes?" She handed me a tissue and I blew my nose.

"Mrs. Weaver, your mother is back." She kept her voice low.

"Back?"

"Yes, we revived her."

"My God, how long has it been?" I looked at my watch. We'd been grieving together in that room for at least fifteen minutes. "You brought her BACK?"

Never mind that we had ordered a "NO CODE BLUE" and someone had ignored that order. Never mind that she was gone for nearly forty minutes. Never mind any of that. I quivered with happiness. She was alive! I turned to my sisters who were staring up at me in open-mouthed shock. "Did you hear that? She's BACK!" I watched their faces, as they began to understand what the nurse was telling us -- a metamorphosis from despair to wild joy.

I locked eyes with the nurse. She was not smiling. "What's wrong?" I stopped and turned to her, while the girls continued the celebration.

"Mrs. Zimmer is conscious. Maybe you ought to go see her," she said.

Garnet, Kitty and I marched down the hall together. When we entered Mother's room, the staff had removed the equipment used in resuscitation. The hospital bed was flat. The fan droned.

I moved up to the head of the bed and Mother turned to look at me. She wore a plastic oxygen mask across her nose and mouth. Her eyes glittered. The jig was up! She knew -- and she was terrified. My heart pounded. She knew I knew. I was ashamed I hadn't told her before. The girls hugged her and spoke soft comforting words. I was mute.

She was in pain, bruised from the nurses pounding on her chest and burned from the shock paddles. Her speech was slow and slurred and her breathing was ragged. I realized her return was temporary, and that the worst was yet to come. Kitty held Mother's hand and scolded her for scaring us. I glanced across the bed. Garnet met my gaze. She knew too.

When the nurse came in to check on her, the three of us stepped out into the hallway.

"I'm NOT going to let my Mama hurt like that." Garnet clenched her fists.

"Why didn't they just let her go? Why did they make me go through all of that if they were going to ignore me?" I was dazed. "Look at her, she's scared now."

"They aren't going to do this to her again." Kitty's mouth quivered but her tone was firm too. Mother's reduced circumstances had even registered with her.

We stood in front of Mother's door like a determined blocking team in front of the goal line.

"I'll take the first shift." Kitty volunteered.

"I'll stay with you for awhile." Garnet pulled open Mother's door.

I walked down to a bank of pay phones behind the waiting room. "Honey, I need you." I sobbed as soon as my husband answered the phone.

"I'll leave tonight."

"She's dying. In fact, she died and they brought her back and she's hurting and I can't stand it." I was close to hysteria.

"I'm coming, Hope."

I went down the elevator to the huge hospital workout room and walked the track. Round and round, faster and faster, I pumped my arms and legs. I needed the exercise. I began to sweat, and I could feel my pulse speeding up. I envisioned my mother's heart monitor -- the weird billowing traces and slowed my pace. After one more loop, I sat down.

I returned to Mother's room after a shower. I had bought a set of warm sweats from the gift shop and my hair was still damp. Garnet sat beside Mother's bed.

"Where's Kitty?" I whispered.

"Feeding the cat."

"How's Mother?"

"She can't breathe."

"How so?" She seemed to be sleeping peacefully.

"The doctor says she has sleep apnea."

"What the heck is that?"

"When she starts to fall into a deeper sleep, she stops breathing. When her lungs are bursting, it wakes her up. It keeps her from sleeping well."

I wasn't sure I understood. "You look exhausted, Garnet. Why don't you go get something to eat and take a nap? I'll stay right here."

She stretched. "I think I will, I need to call Ben and the kids."

After Garnet left, I sat down in the armless chair with my legs folded under me, Indian style. Mother stirred and pulled the plastic oxygen mask down under her chin.

"How ya doing?" I smiled.

"Hu-hot! I'm s-s-so hot."

My teeth were chattering and my fingers were blue. "You want me to turn the fan or something?"

"Tu-turn it tu-towards me, I can't bu-breathe."

"You need to put that thing back on, it'll help." I pointed to the mask.

"Nu-no, it s-s-suffocates me."

I stood up and repositioned the fan. It buzzed away, blowing frigid air onto her. "Is that better?" I asked.

"It's s-s-still too hu-hot." She kicked at the sheets feebly. The nurse had tucked them in around the mattress. I pulled the sheet up over her feet. They were pale white and the tips of her toes and her toenails were bluish. The flesh was cool to the touch. "You want me to rub your feet, Mother?"

"That would be nu-nice."

I rubbed her right foot briskly, trying to get some warmth back into it. She pulled it out of my hands as if she couldn't bear to be touched. I stood there for a moment, and then sat down. "You want me to call anyone?"

"I already s-saw them all." She closed her eyes.

I sat back in the chair, monitoring her heart monitor. The tracings had never gone back to their original, crisp shapes. They were irregular and the edges were soft.

"Mrs. Zimmer, you need to keep this mask in place." The night nurse came in and repositioned it over her face. Mother awoke instantly and fought her.

"No, N-No."

The nurse walked out of the room, and Mother pulled the mask down below her chin again. She drifted off and I sat down to study the heart monitor. After a bit, the tracings became raggedy and Mother writhed under her sheets. I gripped the railing on her bed. She took a long, slow deep breath -- and then nothing. No exhalation. Oh God, no. I took her hand.

"Mother, you have to breathe." It seemed like an eternity before she took another breath. I blew out the air in my lungs too. The nurse hurried into the room. I glanced up at the monitor. It was erratic, but didn't have those scary cloud shapes from yesterday afternoon.

"Mrs. Zimmer, you have to wear this. You need the oxygen." She tried to place the plastic mask back over Mother's mouth. She moved her head from side to side trying to avoid it.

"Can't you just leave it alone?" I bit my lip.

"She's not getting enough oxygen." The nurse tightened the elastic fasteners behind Mama's head.

"She doesn't LIKE it."

"The doctor says she needs it."

Furious, I marched out to the desk and demanded to see the doctor.

"It's the middle of the night, Mrs. Weaver. He's not here."

"Can't you do something about that mask? She hates it."

"Her heart's not beating efficiently so she needs more than normal."

"Isn't there another way of delivering it? I don't want her to be scared." I fought back tears. "What about those little tubes you can put in her nose, could we try those?"

"They don't deliver as much as the mask does, Mrs. Weaver." The nurse at the station was getting tired of dealing with me.

"But she's not getting ANY when she pulls the mask off as soon as you walk away!" I stamped my foot in frustration. "I can't stand there all night and hold it over her face."

She picked up the phone and called someone. I turned on my heel and went back to Mother. She had pulled the plastic cone off her face and was gasping. The fan-created breeze raised the tiny hairs on my arms and neck. I knew it was time. I had to let her go.

She took a deep breath.

"Okay, God. I'm ready. Take her easy. Let her suffering stop. I can stand it," I bargained. When she hadn't breathed in forty seconds, I panicked. "BREATHE, BREATHE, BREATHE!" I screamed.

She took shallow breath.

"Okay, God. I'm sorry. I couldn't stand it, but I'm okay now. Take her, I'm prepared. Don't let her hurt. I'm ready." The seconds ticked by. " BREATHE, BREATHE, BREATHE." I shook the railing on her bed, willing her to live.

A male nurse walked in. "I've brought something to help her." He hooked up two little blue rubber tubes and placed them just under her nostrils. Then he attached them to clear tubing, which was plugged into the oxygen outlet behind her bed.

"This will make her more comfortable." He showed me how loosely the cannulae fit into her nose. "She won't even realize it's there, Okay?"

I nodded and thanked him. He left.

"BREATHE!" I begged her. Hours passed. I sat down and put my head in my hands. I breathed with her. A deep breath -- and then hold. I turned blue and gulped for air. After a half hour of breathing through my mouth, I was thirsty and dizzy. I hadn't eaten for a long time. I went into the little bathroom off Mother's room and splashed cold water on my face. I leaned on the sink fighting the urge to throw up.

I went back to her room. She made noises somewhere between a snore and a hiccup. The heart monitor tracings were loose and swaying. The room was frosty. I looked at my watch. Three, twenty-five AM.

I was sick of death. Why was I doing this? She had not been there for any of the big days in MY life. She'd passed on my wedding, the birth of my children, both of my college graduations, even the one where I gave the commencement address. Why the hell did she have me if she wasn't going to take care of me? Why was I here? She didn't know or care. I threw my purse over my shoulder and turned to leave.

Something hit my hand. It was the Snickers Bar that strange man had slipped into the side pocket a week earlier in the Dallas airport. "Save it until you need it," he had said, his jowls quivering.

Well, I needed it now. I sat down on the armless metal chair and unwrapped the candy. I HATED Snickers. My stomach rumbled and I stuffed half the bar into my mouth. I chewed twice and swallowed the huge lump of chocolate and nuts.

I remembered Mama trying to cook when I was a kid. She boiled eggs so long they exploded and stuck on the ceiling above the stove. I took another bite of candy. I remembered her buying me Little Golden Books at the grocery store and I remembered sitting in her lap while she read them to me. I remembered when I was fourteen. She got a curling iron tangled in her hair and I had to cut it out with Garnet's dull plastic scissors. I remembered her driving me to school on a rainy day. Road mud smeared the windshield so that she couldn't see. She pulled over to the side of the road, and rolled down her window to look out. Just as she did, a big truck went by and splashed her face. She sat back in the seat and turned to face me, opening her eyes. Her face was coated with mud, even her eyelashes. I laughed to myself and swallowed the last bite of Snickers. The sugar coursing through my system, I put the purse down and went to stand by her bed.

"We all have mothers." The man had said.

"Breathe, Mommy." I whispered.

• • • • •

At dawn, Garnet came in. I was standing at Mother's bed, exhausted from breathing. She was pale and the awful blueness I noticed on her toes had moved to her fingers.

"Are you hungry?" Garnet asked me.

"I ate some candy."

"How about you, Mama? Want me to get you a breakfast tray?" Garnet asked.

"I cu-could eat." Mother smacked her lips and mumbled. She was barely conscious.

207

The nurse brought a tray of Jello, but Mother stared at it with revulsion and it melted while we watched her breathe. An hour later, Kitty came in and busied herself with rubbing Mother's cold hands and feet.

"What have you been up to?" I smiled at her.

"Oh, I went home and got a shower but then realized I'd left my toothbrush here."

"So what did you do?" I chuckled.

"Did what anyone would do in that circumstance. I brushed with my finger."

"That would have been my approach," I joked.

"Hope, that's the stupidest thing I ever heard of." Mother said clearly. "Don't sit there like a bump on a log, go buy one."

Both Kitty and I looked at her in surprise.

"What?" I asked, but the moment was over. She was panting again.

"Oh Mama, that wasn't Hope, that was me," Kitty said with a nervous laugh.

My eyes burned. Her questionable lucidity was so brief. I knew the time was near. Two hours later, my husband arrived. He had driven straight through from Cleveland to Fort Smith. He smelled of fresh air and life when he kissed me. Incredibly, Mother stretched out her arms to hug him. He sat down and chatted with her and the girls for about twenty minutes. Then, he turned to me and said, "Hope, you look like you need a break. Let's take a walk around the block and then go get something to eat. Okay?"

"Yes, Hope. Go." Garnet said. "Kitty and I will take care of Mama."

"Yu-you tu-take her." Mother managed.

I squeezed her hand.

We went out into the hall. "Come on, it's a beautiful day," he said.

The idea of a walk in the warm sunshine was welcome. We strolled down the hallway, his arm around me.

"You hungry yet?" He asked as we circled the block around the hospital.

"A sandwich sounds pretty good. I'll show you where the cafeteria is." We went downstairs and got in line. The food looked wonderful. I picked a tuna sandwich and onion rings.

"Hope Weaver. Hope Weaver. Please come to intensive care." The loudspeaker gurgled. I could barely hear it. Was that MY name?

"Hope Weaver, Hope Weaver."

I dropped the tray and ran. I couldn't wait for the elevator. I ran up the steps and down the hall to Mother's room. Garnet and Kitty were coming out. Both were crying.

"Hail Mary full of grace," I prayed. Where did those words come from? I hadn't prayed those words in thirty years. "Hail Mary, full of grace, the Lord is with thee, Pray for us sinners, now and at the hour of our death amen."

My husband put his arms around me. I writhed free, but took his hand. Together we went into her room. She was laying there, her eyes closed -- peaceful. They had already unplugged the equipment. The blades of the fan were slowly winding down.

LOSING PATIENCE

1935

Mama's peppery chili boiled in my stomach. I sat in the cab of Daddy's ancient pick-up watching our neighbors drag Abel Carter up the steep slope.

"Tell Angela to hire someone to help her with the cotton," Abel yelled when he saw me. "Rollo threw a shoe this afternoon, she'll need to get that fixed, too." I nodded.

"SHUT UP!" Old man Baker screamed, holding his hands over his ears. "You kill my little girl and all you can talk about is your farm?" I turned on the headlights. He crouched under the oak atop Higby Hill -- weeping. Randy Rex hovered beside his father uncoiling yards and yards of heavy hemp rope. Was it only this afternoon we lounged on the steps outside school eyeing Mary Taylor's bare legs? I slid low in the seat. I couldn't bear the furious sorrow on Randy Rex's face.

"I didn't touch her, I swear!" Urine darkened the crotch of Abel's ragged overalls as the men positioned him under the tree. Glancing at the faces around him, he put back his head and wailed as if scalded by their accusing eyes.

"She was in your barn with her head bashed in. How do you explain that?" Randy Rex hissed as he threw the rope over a thick limb. I bit my knuckle. When did my best friend turn into a raging executioner?

"I don't know how she got there. God in heaven knows I'd never hurt anyone," Abel sobbed. Daddy stepped forward and

210

slipped a pillowcase over his thinning blonde hair. Abel startled like a wall-eyed horse and jerked away. Daddy grabbed the back of his sweaty red t-shirt to steady him.

The old man's fist caught Abel just under the chin and his head snapped back. "Patience was my youngest -- the light of my life. The child my sweet Louisa died delivering." He swung again. Dark red blood seeped through the pillowcase around Abel's nose. "We've been related for twenty years. How could you do this to me?"

"I swear, Baker." Abel's pain crackled through the air and struck me between the eyes. I wanted to throw myself in between the Bakers and Abel and beg for this all to end. I wanted to go back and start this day again with Patience chattering on the school bus with her girlfriends two rows in front of me.

"As hard as it is to lose Patience, it's even harder knowing it was you." Mr. Baker's legs gave out and he fell backwards onto his butt with a breathy grunt. He covered his face with his hands and sobbed loudly. Abel staggered towards the sound, but Daddy held him back.

I shuddered when Randy Rex lowered the noose over Abel's head. I wondered what an innocent man thinks when he feels the knot tighten around his neck.

Daddy slid down the hill on his backside, playing out rope as he went. He squatted in front of the truck and tied the line to the flat, black bumper. I stuck my head out the window -- pleading. He frowned and held up a one-fingered warning. I gripped the steering wheel. My teeth chattered.

"NOW!" Daddy beat on the hood of the truck. I closed my eyes. "NOW!" he shouted.

I put the truck in reverse and backed away from the hill. The engine screamed. The rope grew taut and then tight. Abel soared upwards -- his head lost in the darkness above the light beams, only his toes visible. I braked and shut off the engine. Mr. Baker's high whining moan filled the sudden silence. I leaned forward and peered through the windshield. Randy Rex dropped to his knees and prayed as his uncle died.

I beat my head against the heavy wooden steering wheel until the skin split and blood poured into my eyes. Daddy yanked the door open and held his handkerchief to my forehead. "Hold on just a little longer," he whispered. I opened my mouth and closed it like a beached guppy -- pale and breathless. He placed my hands over the cut and patted my back. I squinted at him. His face had melted. Nothing would ever be the same again.

He squatted in front of the truck. Abel swung gently as Daddy cut the rope loose from the bumper and looped it around a pine tree. "Scoot over!" he said a moment later.

I slid over to the passenger seat. "Are we going to leave him there?"

"The Bakers will take care of him. I need to get you home." He started the truck and backed out of the clearing below Higby Hill.

"I don't think I can stand it." I rocked in my seat, blood oozing through my fingers.

"You WILL stand it." Daddy turned onto the long lane back to our farm and stopped. "You must."

"Poor old Abel."

"It was his bad luck." Daddy sagged, his muscles relaxing for the first time since I'd found him working on the John Deere after Patience died that afternoon.

"How will I ever face Randy Rex?"

"I don't know, son. Same as always, I guess."

"You were right," I said. "They wouldn't have understood. I saw their eyes. Everyone. They wanted Abel dead."

"Folks get stirred up. They want justice. And they think justice means blood."

I shivered. If Daddy and I had made it back to the barn before Abel found Patience, it would be me dangling in the dark up on Higby Hill. I dabbed at my forehead. Sticky. It was beginning to clot. I turned on the dome light and peeked at myself in the mirror behind the sunshade. The cut was star-shaped. I was sure there'd be a scar. "I love you, Daddy."

"I know."

"I didn't mean to hurt her."

"I know that too."

When Chicago-area fireman, Eddie Gilbert heads for the islands in search of fun and sun, little does he realize that some truly bad people (including Caribbean Nazis) are about to spoil his vacation.

Eddie Gilbert returns to the islands (this time with a career change in mind), and encounters cults, corruption and white slavers to weigh against the routine of his Chicago-area firehouse.

J. D. Gordon has developed an appreciation of the finer things in life: pan pizza, live blues, the Chicago Cubs and vacationing in the Florida Keys and Caribbean.

Both of these J. D. Gordon adventure stories are available at
www.amazon.com

Cowboy Poetry by
S. Dale "Sierra" Seawright

"Sierra's" first book of poems includes

- "4 x 4"
- "Engineer Pass"
- "Home Sweet Home"
- "The Cowboy Switch"
- "Bi-Focal Cowboy"

"Christmas...Cowboy Style", included in **"The Back Side Shooter"**, was published in the December/January 2001 issue of **"Trails End"** magazine.

"Sierra's" second book of poetry, **"No Bull Betsy"**, contains the poems

- "The Epitaph"
- "Cowboy Logic"
- "A Cowboy in the White House"

A Western historical poet and entertainer, "Sierra" has appeared as the Master of Ceremonies for the annual **Chisholm Trail Festival** in Yukon, Oklahoma. He has also appeared at **The National Cowboy Hall of Fame** in Oklahoma City and at numerous festivals and gatherings in the state of Oklahoma.

Please visit Dale's website at **www.sierraseawright.com**.

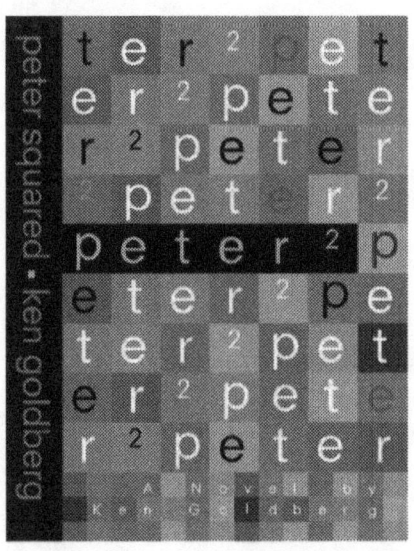

Peter is an anal-retentive young man who lives each day certain he will go mad. He adheres strictly to many self-imposed rituals, hoping to contain the demons in his head.

Ken Goldberg, a clinical psychologist, has crafted an unforgettable character with *"Peter Squared"*.

Ken's novel is available at **www.petersquared.com**.

Charlie Hunter is unprepared for the consequences with a hasty, life-altering decision she made...leaving her fiancé at the altar. Without explanation to her sisters and without visible remorse, Charlie tries to move forward with the only thing she has, her music.

"When It Rains..." captures the essence of the intense journey that only real life can deliver.

Majorie Spoto's novel is available at **www.amazon.com**.

If you want to write for a living, check out the timely tips about the industry in *"Secrets of the Professional Freelancer"*.

Bev Walton-Porter, as editor of *"Scribe & Quill"*, has first-hand knowledge of the industry that has an insatiable appetite but can be very picky.

Bev's freelance secrets are available at
www.ScribeQuill.com.

Here's a travel adventure that underscores the meaning.

Dominick Miserandino runs the online publication, TheCelebirtyCafe.com, and chronicles his married life with this work and other story collections.

Dominick's survival guide is available at **www.amazon.com.**

About the Author

Joyce Faulkner is a freelance writer living in Pittsburgh, Pennsylvania. She studied writing at the University of Arkansas and holds a degree in Chemical Engineering from the University of Pittsburgh and an MBA from Cleveland State. Her professional interests include Knowledge Management, Business Process Engineering, eCommerce and Internet Marketing. Her private passions include aviation, history, travel and philosophy. *Losing Patience* is her first collection of short fiction. She is at work on several novels.